John Simmons spent half his working life as a local government entertainments manager and the other half as an antiques dealer. He always wanted to write and his first novel 'The Town Clerk' was well received and critically acclaimed. The follow-up novel 'Goodbye Sean' starts in the antiques trade, embraces a Government Minister and takes in two assassinations and a steamy romance.

John Simmons is passionate about Barnsley Football Club, gambling, his family, his church and his dinner – not necessarily in that order!

GOODBYE SEAN

This book is dedicated to my large extended family

John Simmons

GOODBYE SEAN

AUSTIN MACAULEY
PUBLISHERS LTD.

ISBN 9781849633574

www.austinmacauley.com

First Published (2013)
Austin Macauley Publishers Ltd.
25 Canada Square
Canary Wharf
London
E14 5LB

Printed and Bound in Great Britain

Contents

CHAPTER ONE

THE GRUBACHS ATTRIBUTION

Michael Oliphant picked up the catalogue for the Miller & Lee auction and put it in his briefcase. He bade farewell to his secretary "I'm off to make my fortune….." and jumped into his Land Rover. This was his usual throwaway line. Perhaps this would be the day when it really happened.

Very slowly, he drove the winding lanes of Derbyshire, enjoying the late autumn sunshine and marvelling at the russet tones of the foliage. He had an empathy with the artists who could translate these colours onto the canvas. He drove for about ten miles before joining the M1, and then put his foot down on the accelerator. One hour later, he was off the motorway driving down similar lanes, this time in North Yorkshire, seeking the auction sale under the auspices of Miller & Lee.

Ackroyd-in-Nidderdale took some finding, but as he neared the village, Michael Oliphant noticed that the sale had been signposted by the auctioneers. Miller & Lee were obviously out of their depth for the signs said 'TO THE LIVESTOCK AUCTION' – "livestock" had been over posted by 'FINE ART', but some slips had blown off in the wind and were back to 'LIVESTOCK'. The country auctioneers had been commissioned to sell the contents of the local manor house, Serlaby Hall but had decided that it was beyond their expertise and it was now "in association with Christaby & Co". The London salesroom had sent four of its consultants to help with the attributions, and also to provide the rostrum auctioneers. Michael Oliphant chuckled as his mind went back four years…

He was at a picture sale in the West Country and he had driven a four hundred mile round trip for just one lot, which he didn't get because it was too dear. He was mildly disappointed but gone were the days when he would buy half-a-dozen "potboilers" in an attempt to cover his expenses. He would usually sell one straightaway, and the other five would hang around forever. So he bought a bacon sandwich from the mobile caterer and sidled back into the saleroom, paying little attention until the auctioneer put up lot 820.

"Manner of Jenkins," said the auctioneer, and the porter hoisted high a gloomy oil painting of a northern street scene. Michael had seen the painting at the viewing. In accordance with auctioneers parlance the description "manner of Jenkins" means that they believe that Wilfred Jenkins may have painted it or, more likely, it was a copy of or the work of one of his pupils with some input from the master, John Atkinson Grimshaw. When Michael Oliphant had looked at it at the viewing, he thought it was better than a Jenkins; there was something indefinable about it, it as unsigned which was rare for a Jenkins, and he thought he could discern Leeds on the back stretcher in pencil. And Leeds was where John Atkinson Grimshaw did the majority of his work, so perhaps…

"Manner of Jenkins," said the auctioneer again. There was a torpid stupor over the room, and there was absolutely no interest from the many art dealers present.

"Do I hear £200?… Well, £100?… No? No interest? Come on, it's a well-crafted picture… Bid me fifty and I'll knock it down…"

Michael moved his catalogue; it was the only movement in the room and the hammer came down. "Manner of Jenkins," he said for the third time, "sold for £50. Thank you, Mr. Oliphant."

Michael Oliphant did not get excited, but he had the feeling that this could just be a 'result' for him. What he did not know was that 'Manner of Jenkins' was to lead to an incredible sequence of events that were to change his life. He picked up his painting from the pay office, chucked his half-eaten bacon sandwich into the bin, got into his Land Rover and drove back to Derbyshire. He left the picture in his car for he wasn't too worried that it might be stolen and, in the morning he brought it into his office and slid it behind the chiffonier. There it stayed for about a month until, one morning, Reg the Runner came to call. Now, Reg the Runner was a very clever man but if anyone had failed to fulfil his potential it was Reg the Runner. In the antiques trade there are a body of men who get a living from 'running', which means going from doorstep to doorstep and dealer to dealer, running their wares. They have neither the inclination, nor the passion, to own a shop or a gallery, and they value the freedom that running gives. Most are Irish and you'll see them around all the time, except when Cheltenham races are on.

Every month or so, Reg the Runner would call on Michael Oliphant with a van full of furniture, paintings and other interesting objects. There would be no dealing between the two men; Reg would name his price and Michael would pay it. It had to be cash, of course, but Michael always did well from his purchases from Reg the Runner and would expect to continue doing so, for as Reg said, "You'll be well satisfied with that lot, sir, it is good and interesting and profitable stuff… As usual, sir, I always say that you only do one bum deal,"

"Yes," said Michael Oliphant, "you say that every time…"

Reg had many qualities. He could "freshen up" paintings, he could source period oak or mahogany for furniture that needed a miracle and he was also well known as in itinerant porter at the country house sales. Although he was Reginald, he was as Irish as a peat bog, and his Gaelic lilt and delicious sense of humour lit up many a conversation.

So, one day four years ago Reg the Runner paid one of his regular visits to Select Interiors, Michael Oliphant's showroom in rural Derbyshire. He unloaded and came to the office for his money.

After his usual, "You'll do well with that lot, sir," he said, "now is there anything else I could be after doing for you, sir?"

"No, I don't think there is, Reg… But, one moment, perhaps there is." And he walked across the office and took the unframed Manner of Jenkins from behind the chiffonier.

"What do you think, Reg?" Reg the Runner held the canvas at arm's length, squinted his eyes, turned to the window to catch the light and finally turned it verso and examined the canvas at the back.

"What do you think?"

"I think it's better than a Jenkins but not quite a Grimshaw…"

"Could it be?" enquired Michael Oliphant.

Reg smiled. "It could be, sir, with a little bit of help from Reginald here. As I see it, there are three good things about it. One it is unframed but it is a standard size, thirty by twenty. Inches, sir, not these modern measurements like kilograms. It needs a heavy and expensive-looking gilt frame. You see, sir, no one ever put a good picture in a crap frame, so when it goes into a majestic frame it says to you, 'look at me, sir, don't I look grand eh, sir?'". He laughed. "The second thing it needs is a signature. That should not be too difficult because, if I remember right, John Atkinson Grimshaw is fairly straightforward to do... Although one Sexton Blaker I knew used acrylic paint and completely knackered it himself, for it showed up under ultraviolet light. And added to that mistake, he also put a date after the signature that was three years after the artist had died – no wonder he went down for eighteen months. I won't be that silly, for I have a paint box full of tubes of old oil paints – some of the colours have long been out of fashion, so no problem there. And the third thing it needs is a location. And here I can be particularly clever, for I have a Kelly's Directory for 1889 for Leeds so something like Pack Horse Green, Birstall would seem appropriate... I think I've seen that place-name on one of Grimshaw's before. Anyway I'll check it in my Kelly's – now there's a good Irish name, sir, so it's bound to be lucky. It'll need a good clean – do you know, sir, that soap and water are the best for it? Forget about all these modern solvents that they advertise. I think that it may need a couple of lamp-posts to draw your eye to the centre of the picture and a watery moon and... hey-ho job's a good 'un, as they say. Shall I do it for you?"

"You shall, indeed, Reg. Take it away and do your doctoring, and I shall look for a good gilt twenty by thirty frame to amplify it."

So Reg the Runner put it between two pieces of flattened cardboard from Bell's Whiskey – he didn't trust bubble wrap and hadn't torn a canvas yet – and stored it behind the driver's seat of his pick-up truck. No fee had been mentioned, it never had been in all the time he had been dealing with Michael Oliphant. He backed out of the compound and motored the short distance to his smallholding at Monsal Ridge, where he drove round the back of the pig sty and let himself into the back of the building.

Seamus Flynn Reginald O'Dwyer, always known as Reg the Runner, had owned the field for over thirty years. He never paid rates on the building "You see, sir, it's an agricultural holding," he had told the Rates Revenue Officer. "There's just a couple of pigs in the sty, a goat called Gerald and some free range hens".

But things were not quite as they looked, for behind the pigsty, the back half was his workshop, immaculately fitted out so that he could fix up his period furniture and with his easel, racks, palette and paints to facilitate his Sexton Blaking. Gerald the goat was his Security Officer, and he had never had an intruder. He lived in an adjacent luxury traveller's caravan. The Rates Revenue Officer, having failed to extract a bean from Reg to bolster the finances of the Matlock Rural District Council and its successor authorities, had told his fellow Council officer, the Planning Enforcement man, and suggested that he pay Reg a visit.

"I'm an itinerant," Reg had told the planner. "The caravan's never here for any length of time, sir."

"Well, you are only allowed to stay for three months at a time," said the weasel faced Planning Enforcement Officer. "Any more than that and you would have to apply for planning permission which, if granted, would entail your having to pay rates and water rates."

"I'll remember that, sir."

And thereafter, he hitched up the caravan when two months and twenty nine days had elapsed, pulled it through the gates of the smallholding and spent the night at the side of the road, returning first thing the next morning. This farce had been enacted for thirty years, and the Rates Revenue Officer and the Planning Enforcement Officer had long given up calling and had admitted defeat. Game, set and match to Seamus Flynn Reginald O'Dwyer – but Reg did not trust them, and a large sign over his workbench showed the date when Reg was due for another night at the roadside. So this ideal arrangement continued over the years. Water was no problem, for there was spring at the back of the enclosure through which flowed clear icy-cold water which had filtered through the seams of a redundant slate quarry. In hot weather, the pigs were a bit of a problem with their smell, but Reg's antidote comprised of Guinness and Bushmill's whiskey.

"Best medicine." Reg said regularly. A power shower in the luxury caravan kept him clean, but sometimes he availed himself of the facilities at Matlock Bath where he luxuriated in the public sauna. "That's just what the Council should be providing," he would espouse from time-to-time, although the irony of this situation was lost on Reg, for if everyone had his cavalier attitude to rate paying, no Councils would be able to provide any services at all.

So Reg put the Manner of Jenkins on an easel in his workshop behind the pigsty. For about a week he squinted at it and tried to imagine how it could become a Grimshaw. It gradually became clearer in his mind. It had been a throwaway line when he had mentioned the lamp-posts and the watery moon but, as he gazed at the canvas, he could see these being introduced, the lamp-post casting an eerie glow on the street. It was from the back of his recollection department that he remembered that Grimshaw often had the back of a trap disappearing in the distance, so he sketched that in on the cartoon he was now compiling. He was now ready to complete the metamorphosis from Jenkins to Grimshaw when he had a brainwave about the streetlamps. What if they had a lamplighter illuminating them? Surely a touch of genius – but, hold on, his previous attempts at figural painting had been rather Lowry-esque, so he demurred – and then remembered that he had something that would fit the bill in one of his many art books. So he got down a folio of the *Cries of London* and there it was, the old lamplighter. It was practically the right size and just needed a little downscaling. What a bit of luck; he must seize the moment, he had already filled in the few holes and blemishes with impasto so, straightaway, in less than an hour, Jenkins was transmogrified into John Atkinson Grimshaw. It was now ready for the caption, so he verified Pack Horse Green, Birstall from Kelly's Directory and copied John Atkinson Grimshaw's 89 from the *Dictionary of Victorian Painters* by Christopher Wood, using the Rowney oils in his palette box. He gave the whole canvas two coats of tempera varnish to fix it, and when it had dried leaned it in front of his wood-burning stove to induce a crackling to the varnish. He then left it on the easel for two weeks before taking it back to Michael Oliphant.

"Well, Reg, that is very, very good. Reg, it's marvellous. You've missed your vocation. Reg, what do I owe you?"

"Just give me a wunner (£100) – that'll be fine, sir."

Michael could not wait to get his wallet out and pay Reg. "Here's your century, Reg, but I promise you that there will be a good bonus for you if I manage to place it well. I just hope that I can find an appropriate frame on my travels – one that will do justice to Mr. Sexton Blake." They both laughed and Michael replaced the canvas behind the chiffonier.

It took six weeks. He was at an art sale in London when his breath was taken away by the best rococo ornate gilt frame that he had seen for many years.

"Do you know, it looks just right…," he said to himself as he rummaged in his pocket for his tape measure. The frame measured exactly thirty by twenty inches. Things got even better, because housed in the frame was one of the most boring pastel portraits that he had ever seen. Apparently it came from the estate of Harry Brown, a local amateur artist. Now, Harry Brown owned some Thames-side wharves in Rotherhithe and Bermondsey, but he also fancied himself as an artist and he had painted his extended family and also their pet dogs. They were awful; the dogs looked like donkeys, but Harry Brown had framed them in an exquisite setting far above the worth of the pastel. It rather gave a lie to Reg the Runner's assertion that "nobody ever put a crap picture in a majestic frame," because Harry Brown certainly did. So, when Lot 72 was offered, Michael Oliphant prayed that no other dealers present had a "dodgy Grimshaw" needing a majestic frame. In the event, they didn't, and Michael Oliphant was happy to pay £180 for Lot 72. He was so happy that he collected the lot and dodged the rush-hour traffic back to Derbyshire, not even waiting for the picture that he had really gone to buy.

He arrived back just before Select Interiors closed for the day.

"Leave the workshop open," he said to his manager. "I've a little job I want to do."

Excitedly, he unloaded Lot 72 onto a bench and went into his office to get the Jenkins/Atkinson Grimshaw unframed oil of Pack Horse Green, Birstall from behind the chiffonier. He placed it carefully onto the back of the Harry Brown pastel which he had put face-downwards on the bench.

"Bloody hell, a perfect fit," he said to the wall, and then, "why am I surprised? The Victorians were proper craftsmen. If a picture frame was to be thirty by twenty, it was made thirty by twenty or the bloke who made it would get a clip round the ear from the foreman. Not thirty and a quarter by nineteen and three quarters – it had to be thirty by twenty. Probably if it deviated, he would get a clip round the ear from the foreman for every quarterinch and be made to do it again. The Victorians were proper craftsmen…"

His voice trailed off as he began the task of extricating the pastel from the magnificent frame. Fastidiously, he placed a small square of cardboard under each of the nails holding the portrait down. He then got his bull-nosed pincers under each of the nails and worked them free. He made sure that he laid them out in a line so that each nail went back into the proper hole. The square of cardboard ensured that there was no sign of disturbance to the back of the frame, and the nails looked as if they had never been disturbed. When all the nails had been withdrawn, he gently lifted the Harry Brown out and substituted it with the Atkinson/Jenkins. It fitted perfectly. He then started to replace the nails, but whilst doing so, he introduced a measure of dust from the workshop Hoover bag. He was careful not to put the slightest scratch onto the side of the nail. When he had finished, he lifted the frame up, turned it over to the obverse side, closed his eyes, manoeuvred a pile of booking forms under it and tiptoed round to the front of the bench. When he arrived he opened his eyes and stared at his creation. "Marvellous." he said. The picture looked as if it had been nestled in that frame since 1889.

On the two hour trip to Ackroyd-in-Nidderdale he had pondered the events of the past month. The Atkinson/Jenkins had been behind his chiffonier for all of four years. But the situation was that he didn't know how to price it. There were so many permutations that he decided to leave it behind the chiffonier until the situation presented itself. And a month ago that situation presented itself, courtesy of Reg the Runner. He was making one of his periodic visits and came up to the office for his cash.

"Have you a moment, sir, for I think there's an auction upcoming at Ackroyd-in-Nidderdale and the auctioneers Miller & Lee are out of their depth. They are really livestock auctioneers but they have fallen on their feet being asked to sell the contents of Serlaby Hall. As you know, sir, occasionally I am retained to help at country house sales… You see, sir, they need someone trustworthy…" He paused, winked his eye and smiled broadly; it was the Irish coming out in him. "They've got Christaby's coming up from London to do the fine stuff and me and a couple of mates are dong the chattels. I've had a look round and I think there may be a 'sleeper' in there. The London lads have attributed it to Carlo Grubachs, but I'm not so sure. I've got a feeling in my water that it could be something really special. It'll keep its nose under the parapet. Ackroyd-in-Nidderdale is not exactly Bond Street, and I wouldn't be surprised if you were the strongest dealer there. So note that one… The sale is on November the 12th. Secondly have you still got the Atkinson/Jenkins oil? I'll tell you why, sir. There are some decent lumps in the sale but they've asked if I can ferret out a few quality pieces – in strictest confidence, you understand – to supplement the contents of Serlaby Hall. You see, Miller & Lee want to make it worthwhile for the 'four tossers' – I beg your pardon, sir – for the four "experts" from London to come up to Ackroyd-in-Nidderdale for the sale. Have you still got it?"

Michael Oliphant walked across the office, reached behind the chiffonier and took it out.

"Close your eyes, Reg," he said, and put it on the fine Victorian mahogany easel that he used on occasions to highlight his pictures. "Open your eyes Reg."

"Sir, it looks a million dollars. It's quietened down since I was… er, last acquainted with it. It looks marvellous, and what a supreme frame you have found for it."

"Will we get away with it, Reg?" said Michael Oliphant.

"I think that given the surroundings, the timing, the companions and the fact that Reginald will be 'portering' it, we will never have a better chance. It all depends on the 'tossers' from Christaby's – sorry sir, the art experts – from London but I shall do my best to present it in the best possible light and, you never know, sir, it may even acquire a certain amount of 'provenance' if I can drop a hint or two in a London ear. Shall I take it, sir?"

"You most certainly can, Reg. I can't wait till I receive the catalogue."

The catalogue duly arrived. He couldn't wait to open it, and his heart skipped a beat when he saw that both the Carlo Grubach and the John Atkinson Grimshaw were printed with their names in full. In auction room terms it meant that it was 'in our opinion, a work by the artist'. No estimated prices were given. Michael

Oliphant thought this was a good thing, and his mind slipped back four years as he considered the Atkinson Grimshaw. He had paid £50 for it plus buyer's premium. He had paid Reg the Runner £100 to freshen it, and then he had paid £180 plus buyer's premium for the frame. He had then sometime later put the unframed Harry Brown pastel into a local auction and described it as a naive nineteenth century pastel portrait.

A poncified interior designer had described it as "charming" and had paid £420 for it. Sometime later, he told Michael that he had sold it for three times the money to the owner of a flat in the Barbican where it was displayed in a prominent place looking across the River Thames to Bermondsey and Rotherhithe, looking across to the wharves owned by Harry Brown who had painted the bloody daub... Well, thought Michael, what goes around comes around. So Michael got a piece of paper, calculated the cash in and cash out, and worked out that the John Atkinson Grimshaw in today's sale stood him at exactly 38p.

He looked round the marquee that had been erected in the grounds of Serlaby Hall. The sale had been in progress for about two hours when he arrived. First the chattels had been auctioned, then there were a few bronzes that made good money and some decent works of art and the pictures were due up at about two o' clock. There were about two hundred people there, over half were local people trying to buy a piece of history from Serlaby Hall. There were fifty old ladies with sandwiches and flasks of tea, and there was a coterie of local dealers attracted by the pottery and furniture.

There were no strong picture dealers – good for the Grubachs, bad for the Grimshaw. He had been joined by Sean Beach, who had showrooms in mid-Derbyshire, so Michael knew that if anything came down cheap he would have to 'settle'. This was an illegal activity when dealers made a cartel and agreed not to bid against each other and 'settled' or 'had a knock out' after the auction. It was a criminal activity largely ignored by the police, as it was almost impossible to enforce. So Sean Beach made a few guarded comments, but it was obvious to Michael that he had come to buy the Grubachs.

"It's never a Grubachs in a million years; it could be something really good. So, if you are in for it, we'll have to knock it out afterwards."

"Shit," thought Michael, as thoughts of a major coup receded.

He was deflated – he did not know Sean Beach well, and didn't like or dislike him. He had this strange way of walking and was someone that you could not relax with. In short, he did not trust him.

There was a half hour break for lunch, so Michael Oliphant dumped Sean Beach and sought out Reg the Runner.

"You are in for a good day, sir." He lowered his voice. "There are two strong bids left on the Grimshaw, whilst the Grubachs has four left bids but they are all for peanuts. You have good expectations, it is partly the magnificent frame... What does it stand you at?"

"Have you five minutes for a good story?" said Michael.

"I have, sir."

So Michael told him about the Harry Brown auction, the reframing and the fact that the pastel had ended up in the Barbican looking across at where Harry Brown owned his wharves.

"So, anything above 38p, and I'm in pocket."

"And you deserve it, sir, so you do... Keeping it behind that chiffonier for all those years. Anyway, the pictures are being sold under the gavel of the Honourable Lord Frederick Joynson-Hamilton, and I'm showing them. I'll only be giving them a quick flash of the Grubachs, but I might just be doing a bit of a jig under the Atkinson Grimshaw. The noble Lord doesn't like me calling him Freddie; he's already been on the podium once today. He didn't look quite right selling fridges this morning. Got to go, see you later."

Michael Oliphant returned to the company of Sean Beach. He told him the good news about the Grubachs, but their delight was immediately tempered as they looked across the car park and saw a Rolls Royce parking up.

"Fuck, fuck, fuck and double fuck," they said, almost in unison, as out stepped George van Hesselinck of Bond Street, Maastricht, Grosvenor House and Olympia; a man who laid claim to being one of the world's most eminent picture dealers. He clutched only a small attaché case.

"Fuck," said Michael, "he's come to buy the Grubachs, that's for sure."

George van Hesselinck entered the marquee. His eyes swept the sea of faces, alighted on Michael's and he came immediately across. He shook hands with Michael, who introduced him to Sean Beach, and said to them both, "Right, you know what I've come for... Let me buy it, and I'll see you right afterwards."

There was nothing that the two men could do but go along with it. George's timing had been immaculate, and he had thwarted their coup by five minutes.

"Lot 632," said the Honourable Lord Frederick Joynson-Hamilton. "There is a slight change to the description of this lot. There is no provenance with it, so we are offering it to you as 'Manner of Grubach', but it is a nice painting. Do I hear £1,000? Thank you, George... £1,200?... £1,400?... £1,600?... £1,800?... £2,000?... £2,200?... I'll take fifty, if it helps? £2,250? Are you finished and done?" The hammer came down. "Manner of Grubach, £2,250, sold to George van Hesselinck – thank you George. Now, Lot 633."

Six more lots were offered and achieved decent prices. The Atkinson Grimshaw was up next.

"Lot 639," offered the honourable Freddie. "Now, here is a picture to get excited about, a magnificent study by John Atkinson Grimshaw, ripe for your attention and investment. I'm told – show the ladies and gentlemen, please, Reginald – that this picture has been in Serlaby Hall for over one hundred years."

Reg held the picture aloft and pirouetted around to find the best spotlight.

"And it is eminently possible that Grimshaw actually painted this picture whilst staying in the Hall. As we all know, he was a Yorkshire artist and a frequent visitor to this Hall..."

"God," thought Michael, "Reg has gone overboard with this one. The noble Lord could only have been indoctrinated by the Irish Runner." But Freddie had not yet finished his introduction.

"I understand," his voice dropped a notch to give it more gravitas, "that there is an area of faded wallpaper where this Grimshaw in its magnificent frame has hung for generations, admired by residents and visitors alike. Turn it round, Reginald." Reg deftly swung the picture verso. "As you can see, the picture has lain undisturbed for an eternity. Now, I have several bids left on my commission sheet and can start the bidding at £20,000... £22,000?... £24,000?... £26,000?... £28,000?... £30,000?... £32,000?... Any more? No more." The hammer came down. "Thank you to the under-bidders. The John Atkinson Grimshaw is sold to George van Hesselinck for £32,000. Thank you again, George. – Pack Horse Green, Birstall to George van Hesselinck."

Michael Oliphant said nothing. His mouth opened and shut like a landed trout, but he was brought back into reality by George van Hesselinck at his elbow.

"Come on, I want to get off. Let's go outside and sort this knock out – but there is to be only the three of us, as I told you when I arrived."

"Not possible," said Michael. "There's a chap from Darlington who was going to bid strong at it, and a picture dealer from Gloucestershire who's come all the way from Tetbury to buy it. We'll have to include them in. Besides, we'll need the back of the Darlington man's van to do our business in."

"Okay," said George van Hesselinck. "That's just the five of us. Leave it to me, I'll do the negotiations."

He patted his attaché case and the five men trooped out and jumped into the back of the Darlington van.

"We all know why we're here." He opened his case and revealed that it was stuffed with bundles of notes. "Here, catch this..." He threw £1,000 each to Darlington and Tetbury. "I trust that will make your journey worthwhile. Thank you, and goodbye."

He raised the tarpaulin flap and the two men jumped out £1,000 richer than they had been thirty seconds earlier. They had said nothing. George then turned to Michael Oliphant and Sean Beach.

"I won't insult you by offering you such meagre pickings. We've all had a result here today. We all know the work of Giotto..." Here, he was mentioned by name for the first time. "Manner of Grubach; what a twat that auctioneer is... So, here is real money for you." He counted out two piles of notes and stopped when he had reached £80,000 in each.

"Is that satisfactory?"

Sean Beach was speechless.

Michael Oliphant quickly said, "It certainly is, George." Both piles of notes were quickly scooped up.

George van Hesselinck looked at Michael. "Shall I start another pile for that Picasso cartoon in your office?"

"No," said Michael, "it is not for sale at the moment, but if it ever becomes so, you shall have first refusal."

The three men moved towards the back of the van when George stopped.

"It is very rude of me, gentlemen, for I have omitted to offer to put the Atkinson Grimshaw into our little ring... Or perhaps I may be permitted to retain this particular bargain without having to part with any more money?" His eyebrows arched.

"No, that's fine by me, I don't want to own it," said Sean.

All Michael could say was, "And I'll pass too."

"Thank you, you are both gentlemen." He shook both by the hand, jumped down from the van and went to the pay office to collect his two pictures.

The two Derbyshire dealers leaned against the dry stone wall, watched George van Hesselinck carefully store his two pictures on back seat of his Rolls Royce, waved to him as he slowly exited the car park and, when he was out of sight, hugged each other. Five minutes later, Sean Beach got into his Ferrari with a silly grin on his face and roared away. At a more sedate pace, he was followed a few moments later by Michael Oliphant in his Land Rover.

Very slowly he drove the winding lanes of Nidderdale, thinking how lucky he was and marvelling at the differing tones of the autumn foliage, and then he thought that if John Atkinson Grimshaw had painted these scenes instead of is gloomy moonlight scenes, he probably would not be idling these country lanes with £80,000 in his pocket. He joined the motorway and put his foot down on the accelerator. At the first roundabout, he realised that he had made a serious omission so he exited the motorway, went the full extent of the roundabout and drove back from whence he came. He was soon back at the saleroom, cursing himself for being so inconsiderate, and sought out Reg the Runner.

"Here's a drink for you," he said, surreptitiously slipping him a £1,000 wad of notes from the Grubach money.

"That's very kind of you, sir. You are a gentleman. Have you time for a quick tale, sir? It's not as long as the Harry Brown 38p saga, but it'll give you a chuckle."

"Go on," said Michael.

"Well, sir, remember that I told you that the Honourable Lord Frederick Joynson-Hamilton took the chattels auction this morning. Well, I've just found out that he knocked one of the fridges down to himself for a pound…"

CHAPTER TWO

THE 2.30 AT FONTWELL

Sean Beach woke early. He had slept fitfully all night with barely an hour's sleep at a time. He had tossed and turned, his bedclothes were all over the place. His mind had raced all night, alternating between a mental calculation of his debts and marvelling that he had had the most enormous stroke of luck the previous day. He was not a strong picture buyer, so when George van Hesselinck had bunged him £80,000 in readies he was tempted to give up his lifelong atheism and embrace Christianity. In the middle of the night, during one of his waking hours, he thought he might offer up a prayer.

"Dear God," he started but then tailed off. "Nah, it's no good, he won't know who's talking. Gabriel, God would say, who's Sean Beach?"

"Dunno, he's not one of ours," would be the reply. Forget it.

So he started making a mental list of the pressing claimants. There were the inevitable taxman and VAT man so he wanted them off his back – he would take each £20,000 first thing in the morning. But, hang on – they would want to know where it had come from and he'd be expected to pay tax and VAT on it and he wasn't standing for that. The £80,000 was his. No, it was definitely out. He would pay some of the auction rooms that he owed. No, pass on that one; they didn't need any help from Sean Beach. He would pay Michael Oliphant the £520 that he owed him for the Davenport he'd bought – he'd paid by cheque and that would soon bounce. No; Michael had £80,000 cash so he wouldn't need a mere £520.

He nodded off, and when he awoke again he thought about his staff who hadn't been paid for a month, the milkman, grocer, his tailor… They deserved some sort of gesture. He looked up at his herringbone overcoat hanging on a hook on the door, and smiled broadly as he saw the large bulge in the pocket.

Downstairs he heard a plop as the morning papers arrived. Due to his affliction he could not get downstairs very fast, but when he reached the papers, on the masthead of the *Racing Post* was written, "Sorry, Mr. Beach, no papers after this Saturday unless you pay the £106.75 that you owe."

"Damn these dodgy legs of mine, I could run after the paper man and get straight… Never mind. Like Fagin in *Oliver* I'll have to think it out again."

And think it out again he did, for today he would go to Fontwell Park and double his money; he was on a lucky streak. He took the *Racing Post* back to bed and started to analyse the day's card, which would have Mr. William Hill cry for mercy. For over two hours he pored over the runners and riders, then he dressed leisurely, had a light breakfast, got in his car and drove to Fontwell Park. Logically he should have gone and paid an instalment on the Ferrari, for they were coming to take it back tomorrow. He made a mental note to call on the way back.

Fontwell Park was dank and drear, and racing started early due to the early onset of evening darkness. He slid effortlessly into the Members' Car Park.

"Nice to see you, Mr. Beach," said the liveried commissionaire. "I'll get the lad to park up for you; don't worry he hasn't scratched anything yet. Sorry, Mr. Beach, I shouldn't have said that, it might be tempting fate."

Sean let it go and sought out the William Hill representative on the rails. Nonchalantly he dipped into his pocket, took the wad of notes out and chucked them into a Morrison's carrier bag before giving it to Paul, the William Hill representative.

"There's £80,000 there, Paul, count it. I intend doubling it before the day's out."

He had paid special attention to the first race, and the runners were in the paddock for twelve thirty. He did not bother looking at them – the winner stood out a mile, for Tony McCoy was on the even-money favourite and he had come to Fontwell for just this one ride before flying by helicopter to Haydock for the four and four thirty races. All the portents were good. Sean had £20,000 on Call Me Morlais at evens which won, hard held in a canter.

"That's £100,000 you hold for me now, Paul. I should have gone next door ,for Doug Smith was offering 11/10, which would have netted me an extra £2,000. You've always been tight, Paul…"

"Well, that's your prerogative, Mr. Beach, but I doubt if Doug Smith would have accommodated you with a £20,000 wager on the first race at Fontwell."

Sean Beach let it pass for he had made a good start, and Mr Hill was going to pay this afternoon like he had never paid before.

The one o'clock was the next race up. Strangely enough, he was able to use the same formula as had served him well in the first race. Donald McCain had sent Morgantonio down to Sussex all the way from Lancashire, and it wouldn't come all this way for the scenery. So Sean quickly downed three glasses of champagne and went to Hill's to back Morgantonio. The only fly in the ointment was the going; Morgantonio had won its previous two starts on good and good-to-firm, and today the going was a little bit sticky. And the price was a bit prohibitive – it was 4/5 but there were only three other runners priced at 2/1 5/1 and the rag which had no chance at 40/1. He had £50,000 to win £40,000, which would take his "pot" with William Hill to £140,000. After this had won, perhaps he should go home and settle a few bills?

The runners were at the post; two circuits of the Fontwell track, starting in front of the grandstand. Off they went. Morgantonio galloped straight into the lead, measured the first fence, its front legs skidded on the sticky going, went down on all fours and catapulted Jason Maguire over the fence.

"Fuck!" shouted Sean Beach, and to make matters worse the race was won by Yagoda the 40/1 rag as the other two runners had copied Morgantonio and decanted their jockeys onto the turf. "Finished alone," said Sean, as Yagoda trotted into the unsaddling enclosure. "Just think, if I'd backed that shagging donkey at 40/1, all my troubles would be over."

Still, never mind, you can't win them all. He still had £50,000 of the Grubachs cash and still felt lucky. But the next race was a very competitive all-aged handicap hurdle over three miles with thirteen runners all with chances. In his summation he narrowed it down to four, one of which was Oil Painting. Too much of a coincidence that, thought Sean. Putting his pen through it, he had £10,000 each way on The Bulldog Man, which was 5/1 and was certain to finish in the first three, so he ought to at least get his money back. It was here that sod's law kicked in. The Bulldog Man never showed, and finished tailed off behind the runaway winner, Oil Painting at 6/1. Down to £30,000. The upcoming two o'clock race was one to miss. And miss it he did. He shuffled off for a few more drinks before resurfacing for the two thirty for which, like Baldrick, he had formulated a cunning plan.

His system for the two thirty was simple. He was going to back the winning distance. Once again, there was a poor field – the tacky going had resulted in four withdrawals, and only five were going to post. The morning favourite had stood its ground, and all its stronger opponents had withdrawn, leaving Mouses Pedals to race against four donkeys. Sean had identified Mouses Pedals in his morning analysis, but due to the withdrawals it wasn't backable at 12/1 on. So Sean calculated that if he put the whole of the £30,000 on the nose and it won, as expected he would only gain £2,500. No good, risk too great, so he sought out Paul at William Hill and got the odds from him on the distance – it was 4/6 up to five lengths, 5/4 for 5 to ten lengths and 4/1 over ten lengths. It was now time to be brave, so he put the whole £30,000 on over ten lengths at 4/1; that would return him £150,000.

Although the race was over the minimum for a hurdle race, two miles, he figured that the "hotpot" would annihilate and, even if it fell, the betting was on the winning distance, so it did not matter which horse won.

"They're off for the Margaret Harris Celebration Hurdle," said the course commentator, "and Mouses Pedals goes into an immediate lead."

It was an easy call for the commentator, not like the Lincoln or the Stewards Cup which are thirty runner cavalry charges. Mouses Pedals measured the hurdles well, drew further and further ahead of the field and came to the last hurdle twelve lengths ahead of its pursuers. It hurdled the obstacle perfectly and the jockey dropped his hands as he sauntered to the finishing post.

"Ride it out, ride it out, for fuck's sake, ride it out!" shouted Sean, but the jockey, even if he could hear, took no notice and crossed the line in a hack canter, but still well ahead of the rest of the field.

Sean bit his nails. It seemed an eternity before the announcement came.

"Weighed in, weighed in... Here is the result of the Margaret Harris Celebration Hurdle. First, Mouses Pedals price 1/12, second, Blair's Vol-au-vent at 8/1. Time: three minutes and 58.2 seconds, winning distance ten lengths."

Sean heaved a massive sigh of relief and went immediately to Paul at the William Hill stand.

"I believe that you have a little matter of £150,000 to pay me. I'll take it in fifties, twenties, tens, fivers, silver or bronze, but no cheques please." He laughed heartily.

The William Hill man was not amused. He looked Sean straight in the eye.

"I'm afraid I won't be paying you anything, Mr. Beach. You see, you have lost. Your bet was for over ten lengths and the certified winning distance was exactly ten lengths, so I shall be paying five to ten lengths at 5/4. So, please stand aside, Mr. Beach, and let me pay the winning punters." He was polite but firm; he had taken £80,000 from one punter on a gloomy Fontwell afternoon meeting, so he could already envisage a good bonus at the end of the month.

Sean Beach was shattered. Why the bloody hell hadn't he used the Grubach cash to pay his creditors? £80,000 was a lot of money, and he had blown the lot into the bookies satchels. It would have gone a long way to getting him on an even keel.

"Sean," he said, out loud, "you are a fucking idiot."

He collected his car, noticed the petrol gauge was touching zero and searched his pockets for cash. He found a couple of fivers and some loose change in his pockets, a ten-pound note in the glove compartment and some more loose change in the ashtray. It totalled £34.72. He pulled into the first garage he came to and put exactly that amount of petrol in the tank. His credit cards had all been countermanded – he was now skint. When he arrived back home, the petrol gauge was again hovering on the red.

It was time for desperate measures. He resolved to go to Michael Oliphant, straight away, as the morning may be too late.

CHAPTER THREE

" ... HELP ME OR ELSE"

Select Interiors was nestled attractively in its own grounds of a former country house in the timeless village of Crossley-on-the-Derwent in rural Derbyshire. It was the day after the momentous day of the Grimshaw and Grubach at the Miller & Lee auction, the evening of Friday the 13th of November.

The front showrooms were still half-lit by Chinoiserie standard lamps, Venetian chandeliers and highlighting spotlights that illuminated the very attractive oil paintings decorating the room settings. The only acknowledgements to the twenty first century were imposed by the security aspects, as there was CCTV, bars across the windows and anti-rammer posts that ran the full length of the building.

There was an ethereal stillness as a light mist descended on the nearby Derwent. In a sumptuous suite at the rear of the country house, sole proprietor Michael Oliphant ruminated that despite the date, it had been another good day in his life. He had sold some good pieces of furniture: a Georgian torchere, a Regency cellarette, and a longcase clock by James Green of Richmond c.1777, all with good margins of profit. A couple of the deals had been ready-money transactions, which meant he would be omitting those from his books in order not to trouble the VAT man. He had sold a Sevres porcelain dinner service for good money and Susie, his Japanese buyer had paid for a container-full of furniture he had got together for her. Best of all, he had sold a Boulle cabinet that was 'not right', and which he felt he had owned since God was boy and, in the end, there was only a small loss on it.

So, Friday the thirteenth had not held too many terrors for him. The day had started with a minor contretemps. He skipped into his office on a high after the previous day's sensational happenings and had hardly settled down before the door burst open and Dale Jubb, his works manager, rushed in, holding the arm of one of the Youth Opportunity lads.

"He's been a foolish boy, Michael; he's splashed himself with caustic soda in the Miracle Room, and it's burned a hole in his shoulder. I've bollocked him time-and-time again and told him that he must not handle the sodium hydroxide without his protective clothing on, but it's like talking to the wall talking to sixteen-year-olds these days. They all know better than I do…"

"Let me have a look at it, Wesley," said Michael. "I've had a few splashes myself – I could show you a few scars, come to think of it. I've one on my shoulder, the same place as yours... It's fearsome stuff, that caustic."

The wound had finished bleeding, but there was a neat hole in his shoulder about a centimetre in diameter, and Michael thought he could see a glint of the bone which was accentuated as Wesley was of West Indian origin.

"It doesn't look terminal, Wesley. Keep bathing it with clear water and it'll scab over and leave you a nice scar like a bullet-hole. Put a tattoo round it, and all your mates will be jealous and they'll all want one. But, look here, Wesley, you have got to respect that sodium hydroxide – it has to be lethal to strip all that paint off the furniture the way it does. Don't go near it without your protective suit. You've had a lucky escape, young man." He turned to Dale Jubb. "Give him the rest of the day off and twenty quid out of petty cash. We don't want him toddling off to Health and Safety, although we should be in the clear as you've told him often enough and there's plenty of notices around."

Dale Jubb remonstrated "Twenty quid and the rest of the day off... Are you sure? He'll be back on Monday and do the other bloody shoulder."

So that was a mere blip in his life. He was going through a very good period in his life. Today he had done some marvellous business, there was money in the safe from yesterday and in about three weeks time he'd get a cheque from Miller & Lee for the Grimshaw, which wasn't. His mind drifted to any consequence. What if George van Hesselinck found out that the Grimshaw was a ringer...? Hardly likely that he'd return it because he'd also bought the Grubach, which also wasn't. But there was a good chance that the Grubach was a Giotto, worth on the upper side of a million quid. So, if George realised he'd bought a turkey with the Grimshaw, the Giotto would be ample consolation, but knowing George he'd probably already sold it at a good profit.

Michael went to the wine cabinet. He took a bottle of Laurent Perrier champagne off the ice, popped the cork and took down an Art Deco wine flute and filled it to the brim. He took a long draught which half-emptied the flute, so he refilled it and settled down into the voluminous cushions of his armchair beside the blazing log fire.

He started to nod off but sat up and said "shit" as the bank of cameras picked up a vehicle arriving in the rear car park. It was a Ferrari, and Michael did not have to guess the owner as the car did a full sweep and came to a stop at the rear door of the showrooms. There was a muffled slam of a car door and Michael watched the screen as out stepped Sean Beach, immaculately dressed, as usual, in a long herringbone overcoat. He watched as Sean Beach shuffled, in that unusual gait of his, to the back door and rapped on it urgently with gloved knuckles.

"What the bloody hell does that shuffling sod want at this time of day?" Michael said to Sprite, the company cat.

"Open the door, Michael; it's me, Sean Beach," came the voice from outside. "I need to speak to you urgently."

Michael did not need to be told that it was Sean Beach, for he had seen him on the camera, and had seen the Ferrari and its ostentatious number plate SEAN. Everyone in the antiques business knew it belonged to Sean Beach. It had started off as 5 EAN, but the five had crept nearer the other letters and had changed into an S and in heavy Roman, illegal type, it just read SEAN. Michael threw the bolts on the heavy oak door, typed in the security code and let Sean Beach in, throwing the bolts behind him.

"Don't know how you get away with that number plate of yours. Plod'll do you for it one day."

"Good, ain't it?" said Sean Beach dismissively, then his eye caught the champagne flute. "Celebrating, eh, Michael? The Grubach attribution?"

"Well, yes. That, plus I've had a good day. The only downturn was that Wesley, one of my Youth Opportunity lads, nearly fell in the caustic and he's burned a hole in his shoulder. Will you join me in a glass of Laurent Perrier to celebrate our good fortune yesterday?"

He filled it to the brim, gave it across, and noticed that Sean Beach's hand was trembling. A man with £80,000 shouldn't have nerves.

Some bubbles had effervesced onto his immaculate herringbone overcoat, so Michael said "Take your overcoat off, Sean; be welcome, sit down and tell me why I have been honoured with your presence this drab autumn evening. Let me guess... You've decided to buy that bonheur du jour you've been fancying for ages. You've decided to spread your Grubach money throughout the trade?"

Beach was silent and looked embarrassed. He ignored the hint about the bonheur du jour, took off his overcoat and hung it on the black forest bear hallstand in the corner of the office. For good measure, he took off his cap and put it on the head of the bear that formed part of the hallstand. As always he was dressed in an immaculate shirt with a sartorially sympathetic silk tie and it was said in the antiques trade that no one had ever seen Sean Beach wear the same tie twice.

He shuffled across the office with that peculiar gait of his and sank into the vacant armchair alongside the roaring log fire. Beach had a peculiar walk which basically entailed two short strides with his left leg, compensated by a long stride with his right to catch himself up, as it were. There were many theories as to how he acquired this curious walk, ranging from a tussle with a crocodile to being caught out by a cuckolded husband and being peppered with gunshot, but Michael Oliphant knew that the truth was more prosaic, for he had had polio as a child.

Sean Beach was an extrovert, always trying to attract attention, but Michael ignored him most of the time. He didn't appear to have any overt sexuality, for Michael had never seen him with a woman – or a bloke, come to that. Of all his contacts in the antiques trade, he just steered away from him unless it was absolutely necessary, although he had hugged him yesterday, but it had taken £80,000 to make that come about! He was about to find out the reason for Sean Beach's visit.

"Nice flute," said Beach, as he sipped his champagne.

"Came – with provenance – from the Cotton Club in Harlem, USA. I like to do things properly – it would not be the same, Laurent Perrier from a tin mug. Sean, you seem on edge. What's the matter with you? You ought to be on a high after yesterday's result."

"That's why I'm here, Michael. I've done a silly thing. I've been to Fontwell Park today to play up the Grubach money to pay my creditors, but I've lost the fucking lot."

He put his head in his hands and wept like a baby. Michael sat and stared and waited to be informed further.

"I'm in deep trouble, Michael. I am skint, penniless, haven't got a cracker, cleaned out, on the floor – call it what you will. I owe a fortune to the Inland Revenue, twice as much to the VAT man, and I haven't paid my staff for a month. The only ones I don't owe are the bookies, for they take it straight off of my debit card. Bloody debit cards are a menace, can't get a penny of credit from the bookies; the money comes straight out of my account and straight into their bloody satchels."

He took a pen from his shirt pocket and did a quick calculation on the scrap pad on the desk, listing a lexicon of debtors together with approximate amounts. Eventually he came up with £1.65 million. He scribbled the amount in large letters on the scrap pad and threw it across the coffee table that was between the two of them, along with a stubby blue pen with a chewed end.

"That's about my only asset. I've a hundred at home; it's from William Hill – he may be in the Bahamas with my money, but I've got a hundred of his pens in Derbyshire, along with the same amount of red ones from Ladbrokes, yellow ones from Joe Corals and some brown ones from Tote – total assets, fuck all."

"Come on," Michael said. "I've seen your stock, there's a million pounds there..."

"All in hock," interrupted Sean Beach. "I've been teeming and lading for years, always hoping that a big one from the bookies would bail me out. Do you know what teeming and lading is, Michael?"

"Sort of," said Michael. "Tell me."

"Well, I'll tell you. Before I came into the antiques business, I was an accountant and I saw a lot of it. When I started trading I thought I'd have a bash at it. It was just like the long-firm frauds of the fifties; it was dead easy, all you had to have was a lot of front, a lot of nerve, to carry it out. I built up confidence with most of the auction rooms in the country until I got one jump ahead of them. I used the proceeds of the latest sale to pay the bill of the penultimate one, and I built up this facility with Sotheby's, Bonham's, Christie's, Phillips... The lot... Even Fred Bloggs and Billy Buggins in one saleroom. I'm about four sales behind with payments. They really are silly sods; they don't realise I've fuck all. If the shit hits the fan, there will be a queue a mile long outside my premises."

"Including me, I suppose," interrupted Michael. "What about my £520 Davenport?"

"The cheque'll bounce. I'm sorry, Michael. And the Ferrari outside, they're coming to collect it tomorrow. Some of my creditors are starting to get nasty, and there's talk of a kneecapping job..."

Might make him walk a bit straighter, thought Michael cruelly.

"So that's why I went to Fontwell Park today with the Grubach money but I was dead unlucky. Another length in the two thirty and I wouldn't be here now. I would have had £150,000 to chuck at my creditors. One bloody length in the two thirty. Bloody bookies have all the luck. One bloody length, and the pendulum of life would have swung in my direction for a change."

Michael Oliphant was now getting bored, and his sympathy with Sean Beach bordered on nil. "Sean, I don't understand; why are you here?" he said in measured, business-like tones.

"Right," was the reply as Sean Beach finished the champagne in his flute. "I want you to give me the £80,000 that you collected yesterday from George van Hesselinck. You see, Michael, what we did was wrong. There's an Act of Parliament called the Auction Bidding Agreement 1969, which was enacted to stop "ringing" by dealers at auctions. When I was an accountant I was retained by the police to do the paperwork at the successful prosecution that they pursued at Peter Francis of Carmarthen. If I went to plod and told him about the Giotto backhanders then, you, George van Hesselinck and the blokes from Tetbury and Darlington would be, as the police like to say, bang to rights. So, Michael, call it blackmail, if you like but, in a nutshell, I am here to collect your £80,000 share of yesterday's ring. Give it to me, Michael, and I will pay it all over tomorrow to my creditors and you'll never hear from me again. And I'll even honour the cheque for your £520 Davenport."

Michael Oliphant said nothing. He was incredulous that he was being blackmailed for £80,000 cash, but he might – just might, mind you – receive a cheque for £520.

You couldn't make it up, he thought, but he knew that if Beach carried out his threat, his reputation would be in tatters and ripples would spread through the entire art market. Good job, he thought, good job that George van Hesselinck has Dutch antecedents. If they had been Italian, watch out Sean, it wouldn't be just your kneecaps...

There was silence for a full five minutes. Sean Beach then had the cheek to pick up the Laurent Perrier and refill his glass every few moments, saying, "Well?"

"Do you know," said Michael, "I've never much liked you. I could never work out why, but now I have a good reason. I have been turning over all the possibilities in my mind, and it seems that you have got me up against a wall. Yes, I will give you the Grubach money, but how do I know that you will not be back for more?"

"I won't, Mr. Oliphant," was the immediate reply. "You can trust me."

What a snivelling, leg-dragging shambolic wretch he was. Fancy calling him Mr Oliphant when he had been Michael for twenty years.

"There's £30,000 in here," said Michael as he slid the Picasso cartoon aside to reveal a wall safe. "The rest is in my strong room in the vault."

"That's a daub, isn't it, Michael," – it was back to Michael now? – indicating the Picasso cartoon covering the wall safe. "It's not; it's the one George van Hesselinck tried to buy yesterday. It's the preliminary sketch by Picasso for his epic Guernica painting, and it's absolutely brilliant."

"Looks a daub to me."

"George's been trying to buy that drawing for years. I hope it's my old age pension, that drawing."

"It looks a daub to me. Will it make as much money as we made yesterday?"

"If it does, it won't go on the two thirty at Fontwell."

He spun the combination lock and swung the safe door open. He took a wad of notes out and threw them at Sean Beach who caught them and stuffed them in his overcoat pocket on the Black Forest hallstand. Carefully he replaced the Picasso sketch over the wall safe.

"You'll have to give up gambling, and make sure this goes to your creditors. The other £49,000 is in my strong room. We'll have to go and get it."

"£49,000?" interjected Beach. "Where's the other grand gone? Did you get caught with that supposed good thing at Fontwell? Jason Maguire should have put superglue on his saddle..."

"No, I didn't... I paid £1,000 to a very valuable contact of mine, it was the best value £1,000 that I have ever paid, and, indirectly, it was why you were able to take that £80,000 to Fontwell today and stuff it in the bookies satchels. Anyway, I'm prepared to give you all of this, but that's all you're going to get. I'm willing to write-off the Grubach money, but you'll get no more, do you understand?"

"I won't ask for any more, I promise. There's racing at Newbury, Leicester and Market Rasen tomorrow, but they're not having any of that money. I value it highly, and the friendship of the man who has just given it to me."

Michael Oliphant turned away and cringed; he was not surprised that Sean Beach knew all the upcoming fixtures and he wondered which course would be honoured with his presence tomorrow. Or not...

"Have you ever gambled, Michael?" Sean Beach asked.

"Our whole business is a gamble," was the reply. "We use our expertise on buying a work of art and try to tart it up, or find someone who cannot live without it. Our success or failure is entirely measured by our talent or luck. There are more kicks about going strong on the Grubach than wagering on the two thirty at Fontwell on a wet November afternoon. No chance of a painting falling at the water-jump – although you probably remember that Irish oil that went into the ring at Neales of Nottingham, and that fat-arsed dealer from Donegal, Dennis McCarthy, sat on it whilst we were knocking it out. Look, let's get this business out of the way. Come with me."

Michael Oliphant stood up and opened the door to the galleries. As Sean Beach followed him, he was at once impressed by the magnificence of the Oliphant collection. The long gallery had traditional pictures on one wall with everything from old masters, Regency portraits, Victorian paintings – some genre, some maudlin – right through to Lowry and Russell Flint, whilst the opposite wall was replete with Impressionists, Cubism, Expressionism, American paintings and even modern works – in fact everything except Damien Hirst's formaldehyde sheep and Tracey Emin's bed with the mucky knickers. The lighting was sympathetically arranged to highlight the different genre, and it all seemed to work well.

"Walk this way." Michael thought of the incongruity of this remark as Sean Beach shuffled alongside.

Sean Beach thought, he's not going to miss £80,000. Perhaps I should have put the price up. Perhaps I will at some later date.

Out loud, he said, "I'm very impressed, Michael. I did not realise that such treasures existed in the rear showrooms."

He shuffled along with his slow, slow, quick, slow, slow manner, and Michael said to him, "It's not for public view; it's open mainly by invitation. I do very well from it, and it gives me an enormous amount of pleasure. Sometimes I fall in love with a piece and refuse to sell it, no matter how keen the would-be purchaser might be."

Sean thought, yes, mate, the price will certainly go up when I come back.

They had come to the end of the long gallery and were confronted by two large oak doors. Michael threw the bolts open and said, "Here's a different world – we call it the Miracle Room."

As the two men entered a large workshop, they were met by the sight of hundreds of pieces of period pine at various stages of restoration. At the far end was the work desk of Ben, the carpenter, who restored the old furniture. Alongside was piled odd shaped pieces of oak, mahogany; in fact, every kind of wood imaginable, most of which had come from Reg the Runner. Between the two parts of the Miracle Room simmered four tanks of sodium hydroxide used for stripping the paint from pine furniture, and from which Wesley had received his 'bullet-wound' earlier in the day.

Select Interiors had a workshop staff of three craftsmen supervised by Dale Jubb, whilst two young men operated the stripping tanks. When he started in the antiques trade, Michael Oliphant earned a living by stripping pine furniture, and hand-finishing and waxing chests of drawers, washstands and doors. As he progressed in the trade he concentrated on buying period pieces 'in the paint', as it was called in the trade, and sympathetically restoring them. The boys cost him nothing, for there was always a government scheme eager to get boys off the dole and give them work experience.

Michael Oliphant still had good upper body strength – a legacy from the days of doing the work himself – and he kept his physique in trim with daily workouts. There were four tanks of caustic, gently simmering with gas jets underneath, on standby, ready to receive the old painted pine furniture which was lowered into the steaming morass by a pulley. The heavy iron grilles were lowered to hold the buoyant pieces of furniture down. The gas jets were then fully turned on, the solution bubbled like a witch's cauldron and, within a few minutes, the paint had dissolved. The process was then reversed, the power jets did the rest, and then the pieces were sanded down and waxed.

"I wonder that you still piss around with all this nonsense when you're doing well with your 'proper' stuff," said Sean Beach, turning up his nose.

"Let me tell you something. Last month you bought a Georgian standing cupboard from Tennants at Middleham."

"I did," interrupted Sean Beach. "I paid £2,200 and made £150 straightaway – a good deal."

"A good deal, yes, but you didn't make as much money on it as I did. You see, I put that piece into Tennants after it had been in our Miracle Room. I bought it from a farm just outside of Belper, and I paid the farmer fifty quid for it. The Miracle Room did the rest. Besides, this part of the business is always busy and it compensates for the time that the other parts are quiet. The Miracle Room also give me a sense of values; it keeps my feet on the ground, for I remember when I had to physically do all the hard work myself, Grubach doesn't come along every day. Have you ever been splashed by caustic?"

"No, I haven't and I don't intend to start now. Besides, it stinks awful, I'm going to stick to Grubachs from now on," Sean Beach replied.

And Fontwell Park, I presume, thought Michael to himself.

Out loud, he said, "I'm impervious to the smell. It used to choke me but now I can't even smell it. Let me show you what happens."

He bent down to switch the gas jets from standby to full –on and, in one movement, he veered away from the switchgear and instead, like a prop forward, hit Beach full in the back with his muscular right shoulder. He hit him with such crunching force that he knocked all the breath out of him, and he started to slide down the outer wall of the tank.

Michael Oliphant bent down and kneed Beach in the testicles and, as he slid further down the tank wall, he bent down grasped an ankle in either hand and physically flipped him up in the air and face downwards into the steaming caustic soda tank. Beach let out a scream of such shattering intensity that it echoed through the whole building, but the only other person in that building at the time was Michael Oliphant, the man who had thrown him in.

Beach's face hit the waterline and the scream curdled in his throat. He disappeared below the surface and his survival instincts kicked in. For one moment he stood a chance of pushing himself off the far wall, but as he pirouetted around he was hit full in the face by the flat end of a shovel that Michael was now wielding. Beach disappeared again below the surface of the caustic. Up he came again to be met by the full force of the shovel onto the top of his head. Michael Oliphant threw the shovel down and picked up a pitchfork, which he put round his victim's throat, pinning him under the waterline.

"You've been splashed now, haven't you, you blackmailing, cringing, shuffling, fucking coward!" he shouted out.

He kept full pressure on the pitchfork with one hand whilst the other sought out the switchgear that activated the heavy cast-iron grille, causing it to descend slowly towards the tank. His next action was to turn the gas jets to full on. Like a drowning man, Beach surfaced for the third time, his face now bright scarlet as the caustic took effect, and he was now regurgitating the solution along with blood from his internal organs as they swiftly deteriorated. His body was now gyrating as if it were on a spit, but this was going to be the last time he was above the caustic waterline as the descending grille had nearly reached its nadir, urged on by Michael Oliphant shouting, "Hurry up down, for fuck's sake!"

As the grille clanked against the pitchfork, Michael withdrew it from Beach's throat, causing a russet spurt and a rush of bubbles. The grille relentlessly pushed the torso as far as it would go to join the sludge at the base of the tank. As the last sign of Sean Beach disappeared from view, Michael Oliphant slid the 'full' sign across and clamped the grille securely home. Immediately he swung round and lifted a 30kg bag of sodium hydroxide onto the side of the tank and slit the casing with his Stanley knife, causing the contents to waterfall into the tank. The solution was at once triggered into a seething whirlpool, which almost boiled over the top before it settled down into a sinister, bubbling, hissing morass.

He slumped onto a nearby stool. He was completely exhausted, his clothing wet through and skin blotched where he had been splashed by the caustic. Funny, he thought, it was young Wesley copping a hole in his shoulder earlier in the day that had been an embryo for Beach's demise.

Then the full extent of the enormity of his actions hit him. As he sat on the stool for what seemed an eternity, the boiling solution had one further gruesome offering, suddenly rendering up one of Beach's eyes, swiftly followed by another. Michael Oliphant grabbed a nearby bucket, swilled the two eyes into it and flushed them down the adjacent lavatory. At the same time he was physically sick down the lavatory pan and, for what seemed an eternity, knelt in front of the pan, sobbing uncontrollably.

Ten minutes passed before he got to his feet and started to return to his office. He was just going to quit the Miracle Room before the first snag hit him. Why was the tank full? his workshop manager would want to know. It wasn't full when he left work. So Michael Oliphant chalked an 'Out of order' notice out, took the fuses out and dragged a tarpaulin over the top of the tank before switching the gas off. He'd tell his manager a reason when he'd thought of one.

After a while he went back to his office. He had to calmly assess the situation and consider every aspect. He poured Beach's unfinished champagne into his own glass and downed the lot in one draught. Calmly he cleaned the other glass and then methodically took a cloth and wiped every surface that Beach may have touched, although he knew that the next morning Mrs Jenks would clean the office thoroughly.

He poured himself a large measure of whiskey and then, in the same action, returned the whiskey to the decanter, for he knew he needed a clear head to carry out the plan that he must formulate to get him out of this mess. Will anyone know that Beach has come to see me?, he thought. If not, he had a chance if he could erase any trace of Beach having been there. All his staff had been long gone when he had arrived unexpectedly. Bloody hell, he's bound to have a mobile phone – where is it? It'll be in the sludge at the bottom of the tank. Better leave it there; he won't be able to phone the emergency services. They'd only have a skeleton staff this time of day anyway. He laughed. "That's a rather clever pun," he said out loud.

But there's one giveaway – that ostentatious £100,000 Ferrari parked outside the back door significantly marked SEAN. That's got to be moved and moved quickly but where are the keys? Please, PLEASE, God they are not at the bottom of the stripping tank. He jumped up and threw himself at Beach's herringbone overcoat hanging on the Black Forest hallstand. There was a jangle as he hit the pocket.

"Thank God," he said as his fingers fumbled in the pocket and found the keys. What else was in there? A wallet which had, surprisingly, nothing in it, not even a fiver, Beach wasn't joking when he said he was down to zilch. There was a small matter of a £30,000 wad of notes which he returned to his safe, took them out again, wiped them and then finally returned them into the wall safe behind the Picasso cartoon. No phone, you would conclude it's in the sludge with its owner.

He was now calm, and was relishing a challenge. Up until yesterday, the Grimshaw and Grubach had been the current challenge, and now they had been superseded by a dead body and its attendant difficulties. He sat back in his armchair and threw some logs onto the fire. He poured himself a large measure of Glenfiddich, and this time he slowly sipped it as a plan was slowly forming in his mind…

CHAPTER FOUR

THE CAR PARK SHUFFLE

The time had slipped round to eight twenty, and it was all worked out. What he intended to do was to drive the Ferrari out of the car park, use the country lanes through Derbyshire, get on the M1 at Junction 28, drive north to junction 34 for Meadowhall, the giant supermarket centre just outside Sheffield and leave the car in the car park. The place would be packed with pre-Christmas shoppers, and was open until 10pm. He would park up, leave the keys in the ignition and hope it would be pinched. If he had been a betting man, he would have put strong money on it being purloined. He would also leave the credit cards in it and hope that an opportunist thief would think that Christmas had come early.

He found some gloves in the workshop and exited through the rear door. He opened the Ferrari, threw the herringbone coat along with the credit cards on the back seat, and then changed his mind about the credit cards. He did not want any dodgy transactions to be made that might alert the police, so he retraced his steps and threw the lot on the office fire.

Returning to the Ferrari, he switched on the ignition and was confronted when he switched on the ignition by a lighting system on the dashboard that resembled that of a Boeing 747. There was one of them winking, and he noticed to his horror that it was the logo of a petrol pump signifying that the tank was almost on zero.

"Bloody hell, another complication. There's no juice in the cowing car! He really was skint, the limping twat. Here we go again..." and he returned to the workshop, where he knew that there was a six gallon drum of petrol that he had stored away during one of the petrol emergencies. He got a funnel and put the whole lot in the Ferrari. He familiarised himself with the instruments and drove slowly out of the car park, silently giving thanks that there was no one about.

Keeping his eye on the time, he drove slowly through the lanes, thinking of any problems that could jeopardise his plans. His knee brushed the keys in the ignition and that brought the realisation that Sean Beach's house and business keys were on the same ring, so he detached them and threw them in the Derwent when he crossed the Piran Bridge. This manoeuvre was not without its complications for, in trying to find the window winder, he initiated the sound system, which was on at full volume. Sean Beach liked to draw attention to himself.

As the keys splashed into the Derwent, Michael settled down into the comfort of the driving seat and was even enjoying the drive despite the horrific events that had precipitated it... And then another thought hit him

"The bloody CCTV," he said out loud as he slammed on the brakes and slewed into a woody lane. He threw the car into reverse, backed into a muddy side –lane, and stopped the car. He speculated that the cameras at Select Interiors would show the Ferrari arriving with Sean Beach in it and him leaving in the Ferrari sometime later.

As he sat motionless, he wondered if he could chance leaving the tape as it was until he got back.

"No time like the present," he said, for it occurred to him that he had not the slightest idea as to how he was to return from Meadowhall after he had dumped the Ferrari. So, as time was now becoming a factor, he raced back through the country lanes and wiped the tapes of the car park clean. As he exited again, he suddenly realised that he and Sean would be pictured in the gallery, so once again he had to go through all the security procedures and wipe the gallery tape.

"Good job there's not a camera in the Miracle Room – that would be a hell of a horror movie, that would. Now, is there anything else?" he said to the bear on the Black Forest hallstand. "You know, I'd make a bloody awful criminal..." but this conversation with the bear was aborted as he noticed that the bear was wearing Sean Beach's cap. "Oh, God, there can't be anything else, can there?" he said, as he took the cap down and put it in his pocket.

Once again he slowly drove the car out of the compound. This time the drive was uneventful and he reached junction 28 of the M1. He had put Beach's cap on and slipped down in the driver's seat but he was aware of the incongruity of such a high-powered car pootling along in the slow lane so he powered his way into the middle lane. Bloody hell, he thought, it would be just my luck for some bored motorway copper pulling me up on suspicion. I think the game might just be up.

He reached the turn off for Meadowhall and slowly headed for the car park. He relaxed, went round a roundabout and was met by a large sign which said 'CCTV IN OPERATION 24 HOURS'. He was alarmed, so he drove round the roundabout and parked in a side street, hopefully out of sweep of the cameras and thought about the new aspect of the situation.

"No chance of wiping that lot clean." He thought of a new plan which would entail him now being Sean Beach. He got the herringbone overcoat from the back seat and eased himself into it, replaced the cap on his head at Beach's jaunty angle, and set off again.

He laughed uproariously as he thought of the TV programme 'Stars in Their Eyes' and announced to the occupant of the car – him – that "tonight, Michael Oliphant, you are going to be Sean Beach." He thought that he was lucky that they were the same build, but thought that the Beach walk with the dodgy Scotch might be a challenge.

He set off again and was at once aware of the CCTV cameras as he turned into the car park. He managed to keep a fair distance from them before he found a parking space. He noticed that the petrol tank was still half full, courtesy of the drum he had found in the workshop. He stopped, swung his legs around and quit the car, leaving the keys in the ignition. Just in case, he motioned that he was locking the car by remote control, getting his body between the lens and the car lights so that the flashing would not be recorded. That done, he set off with his hands in his pockets with the slow, slow, quick, slow, slow of Beach's jerky walk and walked in this manner for about fifty metres before finding some shrubbery and disappearing into it. Here, he shrugged off the cap and overcoat and became Michael Oliphant again.

His next move was pure inspiration as he saw a giant recycling bin soliciting donations of clothes for Kosovo, so he threw the cap and coat into the bin and thought, there's going to be one hell of a well-dressed Kosovan this winter.

He now had the problem of getting back to Derbyshire without transport. He did not want to take a taxi as he had read many a time of when evidence from taxi drivers had proved crucial in court cases, so he decided that it would be public transport back to Derbyshire. He decided to walk into central Sheffield and hope that he had not missed the last bus of the rural service that would take him home.

He strode purposefully out of the complex. Despite the enormity of the gruesome happenings he was now beginning to look on the whole episode as a challenge. He would need some luck. As he reached the dual carriageway, he looked to cross the road but was forced to step back sharply as a powerful Ferrari screeched past at a rapid rate of knots.

"Bloody hell" he said "that didn't last long…"

The journey back was uneventful but long. The rural bus called at every village on the way, and its final destination fell quite a bit short of Select Interiors' showrooms, so there was a long walk to be undertaken. It was also cold. "Wish I had a herringbone overcoat," he thought. There was one aspect that he had to consider during his long walk. Dale Jubb, his workshop manager, would want to know why tank four in the Miracle Room had a cover and a padlock on it, so Michael came up with a solution. Sprite, the warehouse cat had brought a friend into the workshop and when Michael tried to catch it, it had jumped onto the side wall of the stripping tank and had slipped in, perishing straight away – not a pretty sight.

He was at his desk early the following morning. There was a knock on the door. It was Dale Jubb, his workshop manager. Before he could say anything, Michael Oliphant said, "Dale, it's like this; one of Sprite's mates did a Houdini across the top of the dip and didn't make it!"

CHAPTER FIVE

GOODBYE SEAN

Three months passed. In the succeeding weeks after what he had decided to call the car park shuffle, the story broke on the local news about the disappearance of Sean Beach, 'the area's most successful antiques dealer'. He took exception to that description, but he did not feel inclined to challenge it. His head remained well below the parapet. It was the sort of story that the media loved as day by day, further revelations emerged as to the extent of Sean's financial malpractices as debtor on debtor emerged to bewail their losses. One local paper even had the humility to withdraw their description of his being Derbyshire's premier antiques dealer. Michael was not tempted to step up and claim the crown. Eventually, the national press became interested, and even Interpol became involved in trying to trace him. It was, as one paper said, 'as if he had disappeared off the face of the earth.'

There were false sightings of him all over the country, for he was well known countrywide since he had fiddled nearly every auction room from Perth to Penzance to a greater or lesser degree. At every auction he was the sole topic of conversation. At Wilby's regular sale in Barnsley, Michael Oliphant was told by Mick Quirke that he was "100% certain he's on the Costa del Crime."

He sidled closer, put his hand up to his mouth and said in a whisper, "keep it to yourself Michael, but he was talking to my mate Ivan only last week. He's bloody loaded and he's flashing millions around. Take my word for it; he's been salting it away for years and planning his moment of disappearance down to the minute. You've got to admire him, mate. Although he's absconded owing us plenty of money, he's done nearly every dealer, and every auction house, big and small. Eight million quid he's done the Rooms for... Ivan got it straight from the horses' mouth last Wednesday. I bet we never see him again!"

"No," said Michael Oliphant.

There was no sympathy for him. The bank duly foreclosed on him, his stock was impounded by bailiffs, the receivers moved in and his staff moved out. His showrooms were besieged by angry creditors, and Michael's cheque for £520 was duly returned marked "refer to drawer". Little old ladies who had left items for appraisal were tearful, for it was certain that there would be nothing left after the preferred creditors such as revenue, customs and banks had the first call on the money from the sale of his stock. There was a strange silence from the major auction houses, who obviously did not want to admit their negligence in allowing credit in case it proved to be a template for others to try; they did not want to lose credibility or clients. And, in any case, they were lately just interested in the major collections, so that Sean Beach's money would only be a drop in the ocean for them. Michael Oliphant put his name down on the list of creditors although he had more reason that most to suspect that he would not have been paid.

The days following the infamous car park shuffle had been traumatic. He jumped every time his phone rang, and when the local bobby called about a minor theft, he was a bag of nerves. After a week or two, he had come to take a more distanced view. The police would be looking for a man who had apparently done a runner after getting into a financial mess, and they would be assessing it as a civil matter and nothing to do with them.

Christmas came and went. Michael would have ordinarily gone abroad for most of January, a renowned quiet time in the antiques business, but there was a little matter of the 'cat' gently dissolving in the stripping tank that he dare not leave. To hasten the process Michael had taken to chucking a measure of sodium hydroxide into tank number four after his staff had left for the day. The key to the grille padlock stayed resolutely in his wall safe. The system was that as the operatives worked at the tanks, there would be a build-up of sludge in the bottom of the tanks, so that eventually the solution would become less-and-less effective. This sludge comprised a mish-mash of old paint, hinges, handles, knobs and beading, and the occasional dead body. When all the tanks were full, a contractor was engaged to empty the hazardous waste.

And this time came round on Friday the 13th of February, coincidentally exactly three months since the trauma of the Beach visit. The gully emptier slowly backed into the rear car park of Select Interiors. Michael Oliphant had given instructions that Bill Simpson was to see him before commencing work and it was the middle of the morning that William Stanley Simpson – logo WSS, 'We Suck Sludge' – knocked on Michael Oliphant's door.

"Come in, Bill. Would you like a coffee?"

"No, I don't think I've time. I'm behind schedule this morning. But you wanted to see me before I started the job?"

"Yes," said Michael. "It's about your charges. They've gone up 20% this time, which is quite a hike." Michael Oliphant was committed to using WSS as it was the only specialist firm around, but he did not want costs to escalate.

"We have our four tanks emptied at the same time and your charges have gone up from £800 to nearly a grand. Why, Bill?"

"It's the County Council, Mr. Oliphant," was the instantaneous reply. "They grant licences for the dumping of hazardous waste, but they've put the cost of these licences up and have also closed my nearest dumping site, so I now have to travel twenty miles further to a redundant slate mine near Matlock".

"Okay, that seems reasonable. I notice that you have held the price for four years, so go ahead. Oh, wait one moment." He went across to the wall safe and took out the key to Tank number four. He threw it to Bill Simpson and said, "I suppose it's an unpleasant business to be in. I bet you hate it."

"On the contrary, Mr. Oliphant. I love it. There's nothing that gives me greater pleasure than seeing a pristine sludge tank or a shiny midden. Some of the suck outs are dead easy, like yours, but imagine being propped up a grassy bank at forty five degrees with your hose in a septic tank. And sometimes they have leaked or overflowed because people have left it too long and the brown stuff is lapping around your ankles..."

Michael Oliphant shuddered; he would rather be thinking about something else, but Bill Simpson was warming to his theme.

"I started in this business five years ago with only one bowser. Now I have six and I'm known all over the county. Everyone knows my logo, I suppose you've caught on that they are my initials William Stanley Simpson – WSS – We Suck Sludge. Clever, isn't it, Mr. Oliphant? Everyone remembers it. I feel a real success in life."

"So where is my sludge bound for?" asked Michael.

"It's going to the new site at Matlock. I plan my day like a military operation. When I leave you today, I have four middens and three septic tanks to empty, I know to the nearest turd" - Michael sniggered under his breath – "how much the bowser will hold. Then I drive to the redundant slate mine and it's all pumped into a redundant seam and then..."

Michael Oliphant interrupted the flow. "Bill, your enthusiasm is infectious, but I think I shall stick to antiques. You can go ahead with the job, and call back for your cheque when you've finished."

William Stanley Simpson got up to leave. He half-opened the door before swivelling around.

"Thank you, Mr. Oliphant, you are a gentleman. Do you know, there is one regret I've got about my business life?"

"What's that, Bill?"

"I'm sad that I'm still known everywhere as the shit shoveller," he said resignedly as he closed the door behind him.

Michael Oliphant was still chuckling, but he did not chuckle for long, as he had two other visitors.

His secretary Irene Mann came straight in and said, "There's two policemen to see you. They seem fairly senior. I don't think it's the routine monthly nicked list."

"Bring them in straightaway." As a shudder went through him, Irene returned with Detective Superintendent Plumfoot and his sidekick Sergeant Moor.

"Please sit down, gentlemen. I think we last met when there was a scare about a possible large-scale heist at Chatsworth House. Good job it did not materialise."

"Aye," said Superintendent Plumfoot. "We managed to lock up a few minor villains for conspiracy, but the prime movers got away. We know who they are but can't prove anything. They are clever crooks, and always keep at arm's length. Look, I'll come straight to the point, Mr. Oliphant. I want to talk to you about Sean Beach."

Michael said nothing; he couldn't because his throat had contracted.

"As you probably know, he's disappeared. You'll have read about it, and doubtless the antiques trade is talking about it?"

Michael's equilibrium quickly returned, for he had long expected to be visited. The wonder was why it had taken so long.

Casually, Plumfoot explained, "We didn't get involved for some time because we felt it was essentially a civil matter, but now it transpires that Beach had been a naughty boy and there's a large scale fraud. The Chief Constable is now embarrassed about the matter, and has set me on to find him, so I've been wading through the list of creditors looking for suspects, and I notice that you are on it."

"Yes," replied Michael. "He bought a Davenport off me for £520 and the cheque bounced. When I got the cheque back marked 'refer to drawer' I went round immediately," he lied, "but there was a bloody great crowd beating the doors down. I reckon most of them had greater claims than mine. I tried to get my Davenport back, but the bailiffs said that I had no chance, as his complete stock had been impounded. I suppose my Davenport was only the tip of the iceberg?"

"Aye," replied the Detective Superintendent. "It was a bloody great iceberg. He owed everybody – big amounts, small amounts; he was into the big auction rooms for about a million quid and twenty eight smaller regional rooms for another million. The Chief Constable says I've got to interview everyone, and although I'm getting pissed off with it by now, we've had a couple of nice days in Cornwall and Devon, haven't we Sergeant? I can't believe how the trade was so naive. He owed his tailor for twelve suits, he owed the milkman, the paper shop, he owed the corner shop, he owed his garage… I ask you, twelve bloody suits."

"But he had a £100,000 Ferrari?"

"He never paid one instalment on it. They were coming to take it away on the day of his disappearance. He managed to time his disappearance to the minute, and the shit hit the fan with a massive thwack. We found his car in Portsmouth."

Michael Oliphant interjected. "I can help you with that one, Superintendent. He'll have been buying in Hampshire, and he's got a mate in Petersfield, perhaps..."

"No, thank you. You are most helpful, but the car had run out of petrol in Hampshire, and it had been nicked in Meadowhall."

"Meadowhall? How come? That's amazing!" interjected Michael Oliphant as the police then revealed everything about the discovery.

"We ran a fingerprint check," -Michael nearly fainted, he had forgotten to wear gloves – "and a DNA check." Michael felt a sticky substance run down his leg; he had wet himself. "There were a lot of blurred prints that we couldn't identify, but then we found three villains from Sheffield and you'll never guess what they said when we felt their collars, Mr. Oliphant..."

Michael did not have to feign interest. "No, please tell me," he said. The two policemen laughed uproariously for some time.

"You tell him Mooro..." said the Superintendent.

"Well, the silly buggers said that the keys were in the ignition... Ha, ha, ha, ha, ha... And you know why! It's so we'd charge them with twocking – taking without consent – rather than stealing; the penalties are lower. We've got the three of them banged up at the moment, and we're trying to get them to cough for a few more at the moment to get them off our books. We tried to get them for abducting Beach but, regretfully, we've cleared them of that."

"How come?" Michael Oliphant asked.

He could not believe his luck as Plumfoot outlined the present state of investigations into the case. Then came a helpful interjection from Sergeant Moor, who had been prowling round the office, touching everything. He was beginning to get on Michael Oliphant's nerves, but he kept calm and Sergeant Moor eventually came up with a helpful observation.

"You've got a good view from this window, Mr Oliphant; you can see right across the Derwent Valley from here." Whether it was a police tactic to throw him off his guard, he did not know, but if it was, it nearly had the required effect as Superintendent Plumfoot said, "We've got a good set of images from Meadowhall CCTV."

Michael slid down his chair, his urinary muscle relaxed again and he put another spurt down his leg.

"The three yobs said that he left the keys in the ignition but we saw him lock it by remote control and shuffle off. You wouldn't think that he could disappear off the face of the earth with such a silly walk as that. We spent hours looking at the CCTV images, but we couldn't pick him out again. It was the last known sighting. We had our officers there for five consecutive Fridays with blown-up pictures, but no one could help us. Perhaps we should have got John Cleese there from the Ministry of Silly Walks." Michael Oliphant breathed deeply and made a resolution to look up the service times of his parish church and give thanks to the Almighty.

Sergeant Moor was now studying the photographs around the office walls, and also touching the valuable pieces of Dresden, Priess and Rockingham before returning to the window.

"Yes, you've got a good view," he reiterated helpfully.

"How well did you know Beach?" enquired Plumfoot. "It's like looking for Lord Lucan, John Stonehouse and Reginald Perrin all in one. How well did you know him? We can't find anyone who really knew him."

Composing himself, Michael tried to look disinterested. In five minutes, he had been told the complete dossier on the disappearance of Sean Beach.

"Nobody really knows him." He was careful to use the present tense. "I have known him for a long time, but I know nothing about him. We dealers were talking about him at an auction last week and it transpired that no one really knows him. Mick Quirke says he's been seen on the Costa del Crime with his mate Ivan, spending his millions. Someone said he has had remedial surgery to his legs and now walks normally. Then someone said he has had a face job and now looks like David Beckham. Then another bloke said that he had had six inches put on his prick at the same time, so the discussion ended in farce. But, no doubt, some of it will be true."

"Look," said the Superintendent "I think I am wasting your time, but the CC told me to see all the creditors and I'm now nearly at the bottom of the list. I'll leave you my card, and if you can think of anything helpful, give me a ring. You never know; he may send you back your £520. I'm now off to see his milkman. I ask you twenty bloody suits..." He was now getting his tradesmen mixed up; the job was affecting him.

"I won't be checking the post with bated breath awaiting my £520. Goodbye Superintendent, goodbye Sergeant. Sorry I couldn't be of any more help."

Michael Oliphant went to the window, and it seemed an extraordinary length of time that he was looking out of it. He couldn't relax until he knew that the two policemen were off the premises.

He was startled as there was a knock on the door and Sergeant Moor burst in.

"Sorry to come back but there is a shit wagon obstructing the exit. It's got WSS sign written on it. Could you get it shifted? We're never going to find Beach if we can't get out of your backyard."

At the same moment, Bill Simpson came for his cheque.

"Bill, let the police car out, please, you're obstructing them... Then come back and I'll pay you."

He looked out of the window and there was Bill's bowser, with the infill tube not a metre from the police car. The two vehicles played Ducks and Drakes for a moment, and then the police car roared off, obviously not very pleased at having been delayed by a shit wagon. Michael mused that he did not think that the police would ever get any nearer to Sean Beach.

He had paid Bill Simpson. "There. I've earned nearly a grand, and they still call me the shit shoveller," he said.

Michael went to the window recently vacated by Sergeant Moor. A weak sun had come out, and the Derbyshire countryside seemingly cheered up and gave hints that spring was just around the corner. There was some snow on the hills and Michael Oliphant was admiring the shimmering reflections when a bright yellow bowser with the WSS logo came into view. It was en route to three middens and four septic tanks, or was it the other way round? The vehicle was lurching from side to side on the uneven surfaces and he could envisage the contents sloshing around inside.

His mind went back three months to the evening when Sean Beach had informed him that because he had contravened the Auctions Bidding Agreement 1969, he was "in the shit".

"Who's in the shit, now, Sean?" he said very quietly to himself.

He stayed at the window for over twenty minutes. He could see the bowser intermittently from time –to –time, rocking up the country lanes that led to Aylward Ridge. He thought that even from that distance he could still hear it sloshing around. He saw the bowser breast the ridge. For one moment it was lit up by the sun's rays, and then it levelled up, dipped over the escarpment and was gone from view, out of sight.

"Goodbye, Sean," he said.

CHAPTER SIX

MAUD

It was four o'clock in the morning, and the phone rang at Michael Oliphant's bedside. He ignored it, turned over and put his head under the bedclothes. Five minutes later it rang again so he did the same again. Three minutes later the phone rang, only this time it seemed louder, so he took the receiver off and wedged it in the space between the bed base and the mattress, and settled down to resume his night's sleep. He had just dropped off when his mobile trilled. It was time to surrender so he just pressed the answer button and said, "Ugh."

"Is that you Michael?"

"Ugh."

"It's Maud."

Now, Maud was not just Maud. Maud was Maud, Dowager Duchess of Matlock, widow of the 16th Duke of Matlock. A determined woman, she brooked no protest about anything, so Michael Oliphant considered that it would be no use reminding her that it was the middle of the night and civilised people did not welcome a telephone conversation at four o'clock in the morning. Maud had been the Chairman of the East Derbyshire Conservative and Unionist Association for thirty one years, and Michael had been her Deputy Chairman for the past six years.

"Yes, Maud." There was no apology for waking him in the middle of the night; Maud must have considered that it came within the terms of reference of the position.

"I've convened an emergency meeting of the association for nine o'clock in the morning at my castle. It is of the utmost importance that you attend."

"Yes, Maud, I'll be there. Why, what's happened?"

"Fucking fucker's fucked off," and the line went dead.

A return to the land of the Morpheus was now out of the question for Michael Oliphant, so he got up and made himself a cup of tea. Fortunately there was no lady visitor occupying the other side of the bed, a happening that was becoming more and more infrequent these days. He permitted himself a smile at the thought that the invitation was to Maud's castle, for she always made Michael aware that, although he was a successful businessman, he was several rungs below her on the social scale. He didn't have a castle to invite anyone to.

His second thought consisted of a brief summation of the upcoming agenda that Maud had imparted to him, but since the information consisted of three expletives and a preposition, there was not much of a clue there. And this led to a further bafflement because, in all the many years that he had known Maud, he had never heard her use such terms – just a "blinking" and the occasional "bloody" were all that Maud uttered, and even those had been rendered at times of great national or personal disaster, so the uttering of "fucking fucker's fucked off" was obviously symptomatic that a serious matter had entered the orbit of the Dowager Duchess of Matlock. And thirdly, he thought, the Dowager Duchess of Matlock certainly did not do nine o'clock in the morning, so it must be the direst emergency.

Maud needed a considerable amount of time to prepare the battlements for public viewing, as it were. Spirella was the first consideration to be employed, as serious folds of flesh were cajoled into directions that they obviously did not want to be directed, and then poured into a suit several sizes too small for the dowager. And then the really time-consuming operation began – the jewellery. There were layers on layer, an interesting mix of glorious gems that had come down the generations – some even via the first Duke – and some rubbish picked up in the many car-boot sales that she had permitted in the grounds of Matlock Castle. And, lastly, the make-up. Polyfilla would have been a good base, but one of the duchess' outer circle was once heard to suggest that postfix concrete would have been more applicable. She was not loved by everyone. Anyway, the base had to be added to by powder, rouge, blusher, eyeshadow and lipstick before she could look the world in the eye, and she always ended up looking to be a caricature of Barbara Cartland.

Michael looked at the clock and reckoned that, at ten minutes to six, the Dowager Duchess of Matlock would be just about starting the assault on her person. But his prognostications were subjugated by the peremptory description of the event that had necessitated this urgent special general meeting.

At just before nine o'clock, Michael arrived at Matlock Castle. There were perhaps a dozen or so members of the executive committee present when the Dowager Duchess of Matlock swept into the Long Room and, with an enormous swipe of her gavel, brought the meeting to order.

"Ladies and gentlemen, there is no printed agenda for this special general meeting of the West Derbyshire Conservative and Unionist Association. There is but one item. To select a new candidate to represent the constituency at the upcoming General Election. Madame Secretary…"

A tweedy, pinch-faced lady with wiry hair swept back into a tidy bun rose at this invitation.

"Thank you, your Ladyship. It is with immense regret that I have to tell you that our candidate for the upcoming General Election has resigned." She produced a letter and waved it at the meeting in a choreographed manner, reminiscent of the manner of Mr Chamberlain's fluttering wave on his return from Munich in 1939. "Not only has he resigned, but he has also left the district with his paramour."

Serious as the matter undoubtedly was, Michael Oliphant could scarcely keep a straight face as he reckoned that this was the official paraphrasing of "fucking fucker's fucked off". And the news got even worse, for it transpired that the Conservative candidate had eloped with the Liberal Democratic candidate's husband; apparently an initial attraction had developed on early days on the stump and such attraction has blossomed and flourished.

"It's all very sordid," said Maud. "One would wish that things like this would not happen and that one would subjugate one's feelings for the sake of the constituency and the party." It was a return to the vernacular; good old Maud. "The problem for us now is that we have to come up with a replacement candidate which is probably easier for us than the Liberal Democrats, who have to come up with a replacement husband... Madame secretary."

"Yes, your Ladyship. Now we come to the most difficult part. Our previous candidate has left us to address this situation for nominations close today at midday. I have sent my deputy secretary post-haste to the Returning Officer to obtain a new set of nomination papers, and she should arrive within the next hour. I have to stress to your Ladyship, ladies and gentlemen, that unless the completed nomination papers are in the hands of the Returning Officer then, there will not be a Conservative candidate for this constituency and we will be, in actuality, at "minus one" before we start on what is going to be a desperately difficult election to win. You will remember that our candidate was chosen from a shortlist of three, and there is no time to get in touch with the other two applicants. To put it bluntly, our new candidate must come from this room, and from those present here this morning. There are enough of us here to propose, second and support a nomination. Ten are needed. Your Ladyship?"

Maud rose again and gave the table an almighty thwack with the gavel. The table that had been around for some five hundred years would not have lasted so long had Maud's predecessors been as violent to it.

"I now ask for nominations," she said, and from the meeting were proposed the following names;

Rear Admiral (retired) Herbert Fanshawe
Professor J. H. Butt
Mr Michael Oliphant

The first round was voted upon and finished: Butt 6, Fanshawe 5, Oliphant 2.

Procedure then went out of the window as Maud announced that the candidates would address the meeting for ten minutes each. The Rear Admiral was too old and the Professor too academic, and both were hopeless anyway, and Michael Oliphant sensed that there was animosity between the two camps, so he hammered a middle line. He was in full flow when the door of the Long Room was thrust open and the Deputy Secretary rushed in carrying the replacement nomination papers. Maud then put the vote to the meeting and, on a show of hands, counted the votes and announced the results:

Oliphant 11
Butt 1
Fanshawe 1

"I hereby declare that Michael Oliphant shall be the candidate for the Conservative and Unionist party for East Derbyshire in the upcoming General Election." She then rather curiously put the following tailpiece on her announcement. "May God bless her and all who sail in her."

There was a smattering of applause which was not joined in with by either Butt or Fanshawe, and a few wanted to shake Michael's hand. Hurriedly the names of proposer, seconder and supporters were filled in on the replacement nomination papers, and the Deputy Secretary sped off and just beat the midday deadline. So, some seven hours after he had been rudely awakened by the news that the "fucking fucker's fucked off", Michael Oliphant had found himself, by default, the constituency candidate for the upcoming General Election. The Dowager Duchess of Matlock said that she hoped that there were no skeletons in Michael's cupboard, to which Michael shook his head and smiled beatifically. He could have mentioned, of course, that there was one down a redundant tin mine not five miles away...

There then followed the most hectic three weeks of Michael Oliphant's life. It took a superhuman effort to produce the posters, pamphlets and mailshots. The press were not the slightest bit interested in the new candidate, and the search was on for the philandering predecessor and his paramour. Michael went on the stump and made up to four speeches a day, mostly to three men and a dog. The retiring Conservative government were extremely unpopular and were expected to lose their slim majority.

In the event, it was a landslide for the Labour party and they were elected with a majority of 212 seats. East Derbyshire, however, bucked the national trend and just about clung on to its Conservative member of parliament. At around midday on the day following the election, Michael Oliphant was declared Member of

Parliament for East Derbyshire, with a majority of only 68 votes after three recounts. The Liberal Democrat candidate lost her deposit and her husband.

At the celebration party afterwards Michael Oliphant was warmly and enthusiastically embraced by Maud, Dowager Duchess of Matlock, but he survived to take up his seat in Parliament.

CHAPTER SEVEN

"FROCK AND KNICKERS"

Sir Michael Oliphant, K.B.E., O.M., B.A. (Hons) arrived early at the Ministry of Culture, Media and Sport. He had a busy day ahead and was looking forward to it. He was due to host a delegation from WEFADA, the West End Fine Art Dealers Association, who wanted to discuss various matters that concerned them, chief of which was the Artist's Resale Right Legislation. He was in his element with this aspect of his Ministry; not so hot on media and sport, but he had a good team of advisors, so he muddled though. After this meeting he was due to catch the Penzance train en route to the Tate in St. Ives, where he was to open a new extension and host the opening night of a retrospective exhibition dedicated to the works of Sir Terry Frost.

WEFADA were worried about the Artist's Resale Right – it has only been a minor irritant to dealers since it involved a percentage of the sale price (4%) being paid to living artists. In Sir Michael's trading days, all the big money prices were fetched by the Old Masters, long since dead, so it was mainly an irrelevance. However, recent swings in the art trade had seen modern works take over from the Old Masters and had sent shockwaves through the fine art trade, for dealers were now having to pay a percentage of their profits to artists who were still living, and they did not like it. And to add to their concern, there were moves afoot to extend this payment to the descendants of artists who had died up to forty years previously – and even to increase the percentage – so Sir Michael had agreed to meet a deputation from WEFADA to listen to their fears and see if he could allay them.

Some time before, the make-up of the deputation had been notified, nine well-known international dealers of repute including

George van Hesselinck. It had been years since Sir Michael had met George; in fact the Lee & Miller sale at Ackroyd-in-Nidderdale had been the last time. So, when he was acquainted with the make-up of the delegation and George's inclusion, he had called his Permanent Secretary Sir Patrick Harris into his office.

"Tell me, Sir Patrick, is there any reason why I should not invite George van Hesselinck to accompany us to St. Ives and for the government to pay for his travel and overnight expenses? You see, he was very kind to me some years ago and I would like to reciprocate. If it is not in order, I will pick up the bill myself."

"No, that won't be necessary, Sir Michael, for you are entitled to employ consultants and advisors, and George van Hesselinck has a reputation that will not be questioned. He is well-known internationally and his contributions would carry substantial weight."

"Very well; please get in touch with him and explain the Tate St. Ives extension opening and the Sir Terry Frost retrospective, and invite him to accompany us to Cornwall."

This Sir Patrick did, and the answer came back in the affirmative, "Thanks and looking forward to it."

And so the deputation arrived. They were very impressed with Sir Michael's grasp of the situation, which was not surprising, as he had been a dealer of stature and repute, albeit not in the same league as the WEFADA members. He was able to make a substantial contribution to the discussions courtesy of one of his able advisors.

"Look" he said "why not start a campaign against it by getting a weight of your members – and extend it to dealers in other trade associations countrywide – to initiate a petition to the Culture Minister – that is ME – to move against the European Directive to perhaps raise the threshold limit when ARR becomes operative? You could get your trade paper – isn't it still the *Antiques Trade Gazette*? – to carry a campaign, for I am sure that most dealers subscribe to the *ATG*."

His views and obvious enthusiasm left a good impression on the delegation members.

He had been pleased to meet GvH again – he was known in the trade by this diminutive. He was, in fact, a diminutive slip of a man who was well-known for his dress sense. He dressed in a Savile Row suit and smelled extremely fragrant. He had been in the gossip columns recently due to an acrimonious split from his partner, only a year before they had undergone a high-profile civil partnership ceremony at the Tower of London, attended by the glitterati and a wide circle of friends.

And so, after a lively meeting, the WEFADA delegation left minus GvH, and the departmental Jaguar arrived to take the four men to Paddington en route to Cornwall. Late afternoon saw the train pulling into St. Erth station, porter bellowing in a strong local burr.

"St. Erth for St. Ives – all saints, plenty of saints around here, if Ives and Erth don't satisfy 'ee we've plenty more to offer."

The passengers responded to his levity with smiles on their faces and a skip in their step. So the ministerial party changed from the express to the two-carriage diesel train which almost immediately set off over Lelant Saltings and then chugged round Carbis Bay, before arriving fifteen minutes later, smack in the middle of St. Ives, adjacent to the lovely old church and the lifeboat house. It was probably an incongruous sight for the other passengers to witness the four men in pinstriped suits with not a bucket or spade between them. But Sir Michael Oliphant, on his appointment as Culture Minister, had instructed his permanent under-secretary to seek value for money in every facet of expenditure, and the costs of running his department had come in under budget for the whole of his stewardship. He had run his ministry in the same manner he had run Select Interiors, with not a penny wasted – hence four men in suits on the diesel from St. Erth to St. Ives. There had been whisperings that a flight from London City Airport to Newquay would have been cost effective and certainly more convenient, but Sir Michael came down firmly on the St. Erth connection. One of the girls in the office suggested that perhaps the good old English compromise should have been enacted, whereby they flew to Newquay and then got on the bus from Newquay to St. Ives, but the suggestion was kept from Sir Michael just in case he considered it.

They were met at St. Ives station by Sinead Travis, PRO for the Tate in St. Ives. They had been expecting to be greeted by a fusty museum assistant, but when an auburn haired beautiful young woman dressed in russet-autumn pre-Raphaelite prints totally in keeping with hair colour and demeanour, then the official party forgot any travel weariness that they may have been feeling. Sinead gave them a precise time-able of the upcoming function, and then hustled them into a taxi, which took them to the Tregunna Castle Hotel their base for the Cornish visit. After the freshen –up, the same taxi arrived to take them to the Tate in St. Ives, although Sir Patrick mentioned that perhaps the Minister may have expected them to walk to the galleries since it was all downhill and also in keeping with the sports brief. The extensions thrusting out into the boiling Atlantic Ocean had been magnificently executed, and Sir Michael had been involved in the design, planning and financing the new wing, and money had come from the government, the Arts Council, the Lottery, and the National Art Collections Fund. Sir Michael had also managed to cadge some European money as well. He had used the concept of the private galleries at Select Interiors, and the Long Gallery had been especially effective.

At no time did he consider installing a caustic-soda stripping facility, for he was endeavouring to confine certain horrific experiences to the backburners of his memory. There had been a suggestion that the new wing should have been named the Oliphant Wing, but he firmly rejected the idea at an early stage as he had had an experience in his earlier constituency days when a road on a new estate had been dedicated to an ancient alderman who had been subsequently imprisoned for fraud and interfering with young boys. So, the new extension had been named the Atlantic Wing – a name that would be unlikely to offend anyone either now or in the future.

The opening ceremony went well, and included the unveiling of a commemorative copper plaque in the manner of the Hayle craftsmen. Sir Michael spoke at length about Cornwall's artistic heritage with an emphasis on the St. Ives and Newlyn 'plein air' schools of painting, the superb copper artefacts of Hayle and Newlyn, right through to the unique Troika pottery which privately he thought was hideous but was too skilled as a diplomat to say so. Somehow, he found it difficult to enthuse about Sir. Terry Frost's work, but he hoped it did not transfer to his listeners, and when he finished he received a warm ovation as he cut the tape to open the new galleries. The party toured the exhibitions and then, with formalities over, adjourned to the reception area to enjoy a party hosted by the Mayor of St. Ives, which included local delicacies such as Cornish pasties, local-landed crab and the hideous stargazey pie, a concoction with mackerel heads seemingly struggling to escape from a bed of shortcrust pastry. The delegation passed on that one.

It was an early evening and it was time to relax, for they had been on formal duty since the early morning meeting with WEFADA, which seemed an age ago. So Sir Michael and friends intercepted every passing drinks waiter and, within a short time, a relaxed informal atmosphere had descended into the room.

Sir Michael was invited to sample 'loveage', known locally as the honeymoon drink, which contrived to put him in enormous good humour and which the bar-tender advised "will put lead in your pencil." So he put plenty of lead in his pencil but, before midnight, into this relaxed atmosphere would intrude two occurrences that were to transform radically his life-path.

He started looking at Sinead Travis in a different light. She had been allocated as his consort from the moment she had met them off the St. Erth diesel. A feeling of mellifluousness such as he had not felt for years had come over him, so he leaned against the back of the settee and surveyed the scene. Sir Patrick stood with furrowed brow trying to imagine problems, of which there were none. Perhaps he should try to invent some, for he was renowned as a competent troubleshooter. So Michael once again scanned the scene – there was the Mayor of St. Ives showing his civic chain to GvH, and no doubt regaling him with tales of all his predecessors. There was that fussy little councillor who had positioned himself at a strategic position where he could hijack the contents of the tray-bearing waiters approaching from all directions. There was Sinead Travis. She returned his smile. There was the deputy curator whom GvH had now buttonholed and who was discussing – who knows what? There was Sinead Travis, who now had a smile flitting around her mouth, and her eyes directed Sir Michael towards GvH who was now in earnest discussions with a waiter in tight-fitting high-waisted trousers, accentuated by high Cuban heels. Perhaps they were discussing Giotto or even William Russell Flint. No; it was not possible that Flint would have encompassed their sympathies with his half-naked women. More likely it was to be the Newlyn aficionado of half-naked youths Henry Scott Tuke.

Time and again his eyes came back to Sinead Travis, but by this time he had been joined by Sir Patrick, who now wanted to discuss some of the continuing problems from the wide variety of disciplines within the department. Sir Patrick could not relax and, far from enjoying the atmosphere, surroundings, pasties, stargazey pie, whisky, loveage and company, he dourly wanted to talk about the negatives and he was drawing no enjoyment from his trip to Cornwall, for he wanted to be in his Gentleman's Club back in London. But, as he droned on relentlessly, his words were going in one of Sir Michael's ears and out of the other, and Sir Michael was concentrating more and more on the tumbling tresses, the diaphanous blouse and the tight knee-length skirt drawn invitingly over firm haunches. So, when the conversation was veered by Sir Patrick towards phone hacking, Sir Michael played his master card.

"Look at the delightful Miss Travis. Do you think that there is the merest hint of VPL about that lovely girl?"

"I'm not sure I know what VPL is; it is obviously an acronym. Perhaps you could tell me what it is, or shall I guess?"

"Never mind," terminated that particular avenue of conversation. So, much liquor was consumed, and as the sun went down Sir Michael was able to reflect why the architect and he had spent a long time drawing and redrawing the plans to incorporate a long picture window at the back of the second gallery for, as if to order, the sun flooded in as it reached a particular point in the sky, just as the architect had said it would. The white horses outside were criss-crossing the bay in a confused manner, and some intrepid surfers were having difficulty with the riptides; they were being thrown by the tide in various directions that they did not want to go to, but occasionally they achieved a "pipe", the kind that keep surfers awake at night. All of a sudden, the architect earned his fee for the setting sun hit the long picture window and illuminated the willowy body as Sinead Travis walked towards him with a tray of malt whiskey. Carpe Diem, thought Sir Michael, for was there just a hint of a slightest brush to the back of his hand as she served the Glenfiddich?

"Tell me," said Sir Michael searchingly, "do you know John Opie?"

"Not personally, Sir Michael," was the instantaneous reply.

"Oh!"

"No, he's been dead since 1807!"

Sir Michael was very impressed, for did not expect such expertise from a public relations assistant, beautiful though she may be. She interrupted his thoughts.

"Just because I am the drinks waiter tonight, it doesn't mean that I don't have any brains. Actually, I have a Master's Degree in the History of Art from Durham, and John Opie is well known to me. Tell me, why do you ask, or were you just testing?"

Sir Michael backtracked, trying not to show his surprise.

"At one time before I went into politics I had a flourishing fine art and antiques business. One day a contact in Cornwall put me in touch with an old lady who lived in a cottage on the outskirts of Lostwithiel. She had some pottery and porcelain, some country furniture and some prints. I was havy-quavy about going because it is a hell of a schlep from Derbyshire to Cornwall but, in the event, I managed to tie it in with a few other calls and I made a three-day itinerary of it. God, did she take some finding... It was the days before Satnav and I remember motoring down country lanes with bloody great hedges either side and not knowing whether I was travelling north, south, east or west. Anyway, to cut a long story short, I eventually found the old girl and the first words she said were, 'you're late'. I nearly turned round and went back but managed to bite my tongue. 'Sorry,' I said, and she then produced the biggest load of rubbish you've ever seen. The porcelain was modern and cracked and crazed, and the furniture had live woodworm the size of maggots, but then she produced a pair of pictures which were obviously original, so I paid her a grand for the lot. I could have got them for a lot less, and she was delighted. I managed to get most of my money back on the other rubbish, and I decided to research the pictures and have them professionally framed, and now they are hanging in my office at the Ministry. Both are signed John Opie! So there. I shouldn't really tell you all the details but all dealers – and ex-dealers – like to brag about the good deals they have done. They don't mention the many duff deals that they have transacted. How do you know about John Opie?"

"I live near to where he was born, at St. Agnes, not too far from here."

"Well, isn't it funny that a chance remark could lead to all this information? When I look at them, I marvel at their simplicity and their utter charm. I don't suppose that you could show me his birthplace, could you? It would bring some empathy from Cornwall to Whitehall."

"I could take you there in the morning if you are not leaving too early."

Sir Michael considered the matter for all of three seconds.

"I don't think that there is anything fixed that cannot be unfixed," he said. "It would be delightful. Are you able to chauffeur me?

"No problem. I could pick you up about nine thirty if that fits your plans?"

So Sir Michael motioned to his permanent secretary who came across with a grumpy expression on his face. "You know we are scheduled to leave at ten o'clock in the morning."

"Yes, Sir Michael."

"Well we're not. Reschedule it to three o'clock in the afternoon."

"That's most inconsistent, Sir Michael. It will be most difficult."

"Yes, but not impossible so fix it. It is not often that I am awkward, but this time I have made alternative arrangements for the morrow, so do as I say."

"I will, but I have to say that it will need a major revision of arrangements both here and in London for so many people and -"

His moaning manner was cut peremptorily short by Sir Michael who interrupted with, "I am sure that it will be well within your administrative capabilities, so do it."

"Okay." He scurried away with a highly audible tut-tut. Sir Michael turned to Sinead who had been witness to this conversation, although was pretending to turn a deaf ear.

"That's the way to do it. It is called abuse of power. I don't put my foot down with a heavy hand very often, but this evening I've done it for a pretty girl, and John Opie. So I'd like, please, to take you up on your offer and please, could you pick me up at nine thirty from the Tregunna Castle Hotel?"

"I shall look forward to it. I have to go off duty this moment."

She leaned over to him and kissed him lightly on the cheek, leaving behind a lingering whiff of an exotic perfume.

And so the evening wore on and Sir Michael circulated; local dignitaries wanted to talk to him and he was enjoying the reflected glory, as all politicians do. He was looking forward to the morning, but late in the evening, just as he was preparing to leave, GvH sidled over to him and Sir Michael felt that he had been waiting his moment to get him on his own.

"Well done, Sir Michael – the arrangements have been first class and it was really very kind of you to include me in your arrangements."

"Please call me Mike, George... we go back a long way. Yes, it has been a long day but most rewarding. What did you think of the Sir Terry Frost retrospective?"

"Load of bollocks," was the instant reply from GvH. It took Sir Michael's breath away, so venomous was the tone of his voice. "It's rubbish like that, and Lucien Freud, and Francis Bacon and all the other motley crew that have put the skids under 'real' art by 'real' painters."

It was not that GvH had given any clue that a vituperative tirade was forthcoming. He had been good company on the journey down to Cornwall, and prior to that had made intelligent contributions as a representative of the art trade in the WEFADA negotiations, and throughout the evening Sir Michael had noticed him flitting amongst the guests, dispensing bonhomie, even though he was spending some little time with a beautiful young waiter in a body-sculpted tunic and Cuban heels. But there were two sides to GvH, and he was warming to his theme. His pleasant face had become contorted, and it was obvious that he was suffering some deep-down traumas and that his previous jocular jovial mood had been a mask. His eyes narrowed to a slit as he continued.

"Bacon was the worst of the lot. He tried to shag me once... as if I could fancy a man as unattractive as him! He looked like a bloody turd. Anyway, I digress – for how could people be conned into buying unmade beds and pickled bloody sheep? What are you supposed to do with an unmade bed – frame it into a rococo frame, hang it on the wall and drape soiled knickers round it? No wonder the fine art business is in a state... Make no mistakes about it, it is in a fucking state. Look around you. At one time, not so long ago, every town had a dozen shops varying from fine art through general antiques and objets d'art, and through to the junk shops where you might pick up a bargain. Now there are none; just a few 'centres' where tired teachers display their trinkets in the hope of making a bob on the side."

Sir Michael Oliphant agreed wholeheartedly with this summation in accordance with his pedigree, but couldn't express his opinion publicly, although he had a permanent bee in his bonnet about IKEA who he thought had started this downturn in the trade with their 'kick out the chintz' campaign.

"You are so right, George. I could never work out why the Terry Frost acrylics started making money – they were just geometric sketches that somehow tickle a collectors fancy and his work spawned a whole legion of copycats so that every sale these days has a 'modern' section that I am sure my goddaughter Lola could replicate by sticking her fingers in the paint pot."

He looked across at GvH and witnessed a plum-red face above a bulbous and bucolic neck and froth around his mouth. He spoke in a whisper.

"You know the quality of the Old Masters used to take my breath away and they have brought me to tears, but now they are salted away in the collections of people who have too much money. There is no inbetween. A few Victorian painters make decent money, but these people with unmade beds on their walls aren't going to intersperse it with a 'Monarch of the Glen', are they? And all the major auctioneers are complicit with this trend. Bloody Sotheby's, Christie's and the rest of the big boys have shut down their regional sale-rooms and now concentrate on tramming their modern rubbish around the world – and with vendor's commission and buyer's premium they cop up to 50% of the hammer price. No wonder they are not interested in selling an elegant Victorian chiffonier in Retford anymore. Why bother to earn a few quid in a country auction when you can get a large wedge from 'The Scream' in New York? This bloody country is obsessed with celebrity – it couldn't give a toss about quality anymore. And what about Andy Warhol? How could a silkscreen print of Chairman Mao or Marilyn Monroe fetch millions of pounds? The situation has left me in limbo. I don't know whether I should try to beat them or join them. And most of the smart young men of today aren't. They've a week's growth round their chops, no ties, scruffy open-necked shirts and jeans with rips up the legs and even across the arse. They all look as if they've been sleeping rough for a week. And what do they call it? Style and fashion. Could you imagine? If I dressed like that I'd be chucked out of Maastricht. Andy Warhol... Andy Arsehole, more like," he spat out.

GvH was near to tears, so Michael put a hand on his shoulder and beckoned a waiter to refill both their glasses. He felt desperately sorry for the man, so he guided him to a settee and helped him sit down. It was obvious that the split from his partner had devastated him and he also felt that he owed him moral support after the Grubachs attribution, even though that was way, way back in the past.

"Want to tell me about Lionel?" he said.

GvH took a long draught from a glass of whiskey and as he had only be nibbling at the canapés, his body alcohol percentage was beginning to affect his slight frame and he was losing his composure.

"The bastard," he spat out venomously – and loudly, so loudly that it caused a hush in the conversations nearby. "The bastard's taken me for everything I've got. Everyone knew that I was the talented one of the partnership. George, the international art dealer, respected all over the world and Lionel, interior designer; a match made in heaven that ended in hell."

He paused, wept salty tears, took a large swig of the whiskey and nearly fell off the settee. Everybody else at the reception was giving GvH a wide berth and pretending that he was not there.

"Go on," said Michael. He felt real sympathy for the man – a man he did not know well but had respected all these years. GvH continued his character assassination of Lionel, his former partner.

"Interior designer, huh – he couldn't design a shithouse in Shadwell. I kept putting work his way from some of the nice ladies that I had commissions from but he kept messing up, big style. We had been together as lovers and business partners for nearly twelve years when he suggested that we should cement our love with a formal partnership. He even went down on one knee to me in the Savoy Restaurant. Christ, I stood for it and we embarked on that notorious bash at the Tower of London. Was that only a year ago? It cost me a frigging packet. I tried to sell the photo-rights to *Hello* or *OK* but they both said that they'd prefer to stick to more conventional 'arrangements' and all we rated was a couple of paragraphs in *Gay News*. And he looked so beautiful on the day," he concluded wistfully.

"Where is he now?" queried Michael.

"Do you want the really bad news?"

"Go on…"

George took out a large floral handkerchief and theatrically dabbed his eyes.

"Would you believe it? He's in bloody Thailand. He'd been knocking off a Thai cocktail barman for the past six months. Apparently all the time I was away doing Fairs all over the world he was having assignations with his dusky lover. No wonder he always looked shagged out when I came back… He said that he'd been spring cleaning the apartment, but I caught him out by running my finger on the top of the door-jamb and finding enough dust to plant a row of potatoes in. The denouement took place when I was in Maastricht last month. He cleared all our joint accounts, sold all our furniture to dodgy dealers at a fraction of its worth, flogged every picture off the walls, every ornament from every cabinet, and then the cabinets themselves. Then he fucked off to Phuket with his tight-arsed cocktail barman. And do you know what? When I came back from Maastricht I couldn't get into the apartment. He'd changed every lock in the door. Don't know why he did that, there was fuck-all left in there. He'd even flogged all the Ispahan carpets to a dodgy Turk. Things could only get worse, and they already had, for on the way back from Maastricht – where my takings had been precisely zilch – the ferry pitched and I put my foot through a nice oil by Fronglia which stood me a half a million Euros and not paid for. And then I came back and found Lionel had lamplighted. Business had been in freefall for the past three years. The rent on my Bond Street showrooms had trebled and the owners wanted to get me out to get some chain store in probably bloody IKEA. So there I was on the slippery slope. I came back and Lionel had done the dirty on me. The only collateral I had was tied up in my accumulations over a lifetime, and Lionel had sold the lot for a fraction of the value…"

"Didn't you go to the police?" enquired Michael.

"I did," was the reply. "Told them all about my troubles with Lionel and they said it was a civil matter and couldn't wait to give me the bum's rush out of the station. So I started to trawl through my memory bank for someone who could help me out of my predicament, and do you know who I came up with?"

Sir Michael thought he knew who the answer would be; it would be Her Majesty's Minister for Culture, Media and Sport. He was wrong.

"Sean Beach!"

Michael dropped his glass and spilt neat whiskey down neat trousers. He spluttered apologetically and shaded his eyes with both hands.

"Good Lord," was all he managed to say.

"It was interesting what I came up with."

I bet it was, thought Michael.

"I bumped into Mick Quirke, you know the sculpture dealer, and he told me that some time ago that Sean Beach had decamped to the Costa del Crime owing everyone an absolute fortune, and had gone big-time into drug running and was now worth millions. He is top of the police Wanted list, but he's a clever man – he is always at arms length to any deals and they can't feel his collar." Or any other part of his anatomy, thought Michael. "So I hopped off to Spain to find him – do you know I could only afford a ticket on Easyjet? Just imagine, GvH on Easyjet – because I wanted to remind him of a certain auction at Ackroyd-in-Nidderdale some years ago when I was happy to pay him mega-money in the knock –out, and it was probably this wedge that started him on the road to riches."

"How did you get on?"

"Failed, couldn't find him."

Sir Michael feigned surprise.

"I spent three days there. Everyone wanted to talk about him for apparently he has become a folk hero for doing the big auction houses, but funnily enough, nobody would attest to actually having seen him. It's as if he has become an apocryphal character. Apparently he has had a lot of surgery. Remember that funny walk he had? They've cured that, although God knows how they managed it. He's either taken off or put on a load of weight depending who you are talking to. He's married into the Spanish aristocracy, he's in a Sicilian drug cartel... You wouldn't believe the half of it. It is stranger than fiction."

And so is the truth, thought Michael. Then came the moment he feared.

"Mike ..." GvH got up, swayed forty five degrees, but managed to stay on his feet. "Mike, I'm pissed and I'm going to bed. But I have to say it, Mike, there was another person at Ackroyd-in-Nidderdale to whom I was exceedingly generous, and that was you. Can you help me? Try to come up with something quickly to help me out of this mess, please Mike... I'm really on the floor. Perhaps in the morning you may find an avenue. I'd be exceedingly grateful. Goodnight."

He lurched forward and put both his arms around Michael's neck and kissed him on the lips. He made his unsteady way up the central staircase to exit the Tate St. Ives. Halfway up he pirouetted and waved falteringly before regaining his equilibrium, then going down on all fours and clambering up the rest of the staircase. And so GvH exited the reception. Sir Michael hoped that he had fallen straight into the Atlantic, but a commissionaire poured him into a taxi and directed the driver to take him to the Tregunna Castle Hotel. Suddenly Michael was stone cold sober. He could foresee trouble, big trouble, and he felt that his cosy world was in danger of being invaded. He must not ignore the portents, for already in his mind he could see *The Sun*'s headlines: 'Minister took £80,000 Bung' for GvH knew all about The Auctions Bidding Agreement 1934. He could put GvH on his list of consultants but could not pay him anything substantial, as that would be political suicide. He could... The possibilities were stacking up, but he had to discount a leisurely visit to the caustic soda bath due to change of circumstances.

He went to bed cursing the Grubachs attribution, but his distress was counterbalanced by thinking about John Opie and that delicious hint of VPL. He did not sleep much that night. He was down for an early breakfast in readiness for the trip to see the John Opie cottage, and was surprised and annoyed to be joined at the table by GvH, looking decidedly fragile. His fragrancy had been replaced by a louche 'frayed at the edges' look, with more than a hint of Quinton Crisp about him. Kedgeree was served. GvH caught just a whiff of it before lurching to an adjacent lavatory where the contents of last night's alcoholic cocktails that had invaded his digestive tract were deposited in the pan. A poor start to the day for Sir Michael; so when GvH returned to the table he launched straight into his 'recovery initiative' and said to him, "Come to my London office. I've made an appointment with my diary secretary for ten twenty on the 28th. I'll come up with something by then, trust me."

This date was in ten days' time and was a device to buy him some time. It did not work.

"No good" said GvH. "Perhaps I did not stress due to my emotional state the importance of my situation. I'll come to your London office at ten thirty in the morning. Tell your diary secretary that." There was more than a hint of malice in his voice. His manner was almost threatening, so Sir Michael could see no point in any further discussion.

"Okay," he said, and GvH left without a further word.

He sat there on his own, in a state of suspended animation, for some time. The day had dawned hot and humid and the rays of the strong sun filtered through the blinds. He turned down the waiter's offer of a refill with a wave of his hand, but his demeanour caused the waiter to enquire, "Are you alright, Sir?"

His vacant mood was shattered by the arrival at his table of his Permanent Private Secretary Sir Patrick Harris, who immediately started to stress his continued grievance at the change of plan for the departure arrangements. It was just the lever Sir Michael needed. He looked round and ensured that no one was within earshot.

"Look," he said, "stop fucking bleating, will you? And do as you are told for a change. You may have overlooked the fact that I am the master and you are the servant. When I say things have changed, just accept the fact and get on with it. You have been sulking now for the best part of twelve hours, and all I have asked you to do is swap a few things around. Since I've been at this Ministry, I haven't caused you as much as a hiccup. But, on this occasion, I am insisting we are leaving at three o'clock, so stop sulking and get on with it. And, think on this, if I say we are not leaving until Christmas, we are leaving at Christmas. Understand? Sometimes," he paused for emphasis, "you get on my fucking tits." It was all quite out a character from his usual suave manner.

It was all a big shock for the titled career civil servant, but the dressing-down was terminated by an interruption by the Duty Manager, who came up to the table and said, "There's a young lady at reception for you, Sir Michael."

So he skipped up from the table, thinking that the timing had been immaculate and that Sir Patrick had been due a reprimand for some time, and he did not regret for one moment inflicting it on him. He reckoned that if a man did not know what VPL was, he deserved it anyway.

She looked delicious and he told her so. "Must be back by three or Old Misery Guts will blow a gasket." He motioned towards the breakfast room where she could just see Sir Patrick sitting looking shell-shocked.

She said, "What have you done to him?"

"He was due a rollocking and he's just had one. Never mind about him, he'll recover. What's the SP?"

She was not fazed by the question or the abbreviation. "The SP. I know exactly what that means, for I come from a gambling family, is that we drive to St. Agnes. It takes about twenty minutes. Go up to the Blue Hills, park up, and then walk via Trevellas Porth up Jericho Valley and I'll show you the cottage in which John Opie was born. On the way to the Blue Hills we'll pass St. Agnes Church, and we'll stop outside and I'll show you a lovely little oil by Opie that's been on display in the Church for a hundred years. And, on the way back, you can buy me lunch to reciprocate the largesse that the ratepayers of Cornwall have shown to you these past few hours... and," she paused and a mischievous note entered her voice, "think twice what you claim for because I understand that you lot at Westminster have been having a little local difficulty in relation to expenses claims recently."

And the morning went almost as planned. They sneaked a look at the St. Agnes Church's Opie, but then arrangements altered as he bought a picnic hamper in the village and a bottle of Laurent Perrier champagne, his favourite brand. At Trevellas Porth they parked up and walked hand-in-hand across the Blue Hills, up Jericho Valley and onto John Opie's Cottage.

It was hot. They found a clearing amongst the shale and the grass was close-cropped and springy; it had been kept short by the feral rabbits. He set out the picnic which he had bought randomly for he had no idea what her tastes were, although he hazarded a guess that with haunches like that she wouldn't be a vegetarian. He popped the Laurent Perrier and toasted "Us" – it was a trite offering, but spontaneous.

She added, "And the Tate St. Ives," which was just as trite, but she had a feeling that something was just beginning to happen. It was hard to explain or quantify, but lovers will know what she meant.

"Bloody hell," he said, "the first sip tastes good. God's in his heaven, there are surfers in the distance and one has just caught an almighty roller, the sun is burning down, Misery Guts is altering his timetables, I'm with a beautiful girl and if anyone is having a better time than I am at this moment, then he's having a hell of a time. So let's be selfish – to us."

And they clinked their Art Deco long-stemmed flutes and as sweat flicked into his eyelids the red, green, yellow and purple concentric circles of the flutes gelled into one. Sinead got up.

"Listen to this," she said and flicked a switch in the music system. She left the passenger door half-open so that the lush strings seemingly flooded into the valley.

"Go on, I know it… Or I ought to, for I am the bloody Culture Minister... No I can't bring it to mind; tell me," he said and looked exasperated.

"It's 'Pavane for a Dead Princess' by Ravel. It may have a grisly nomenclature, but I think it suits the mood of the occasion, don't you?"

She sat cross-legged in front of him and was wearing an off-the-shoulder lace top with a velvet pull gathered between the breasts. She crossed and uncrossed her legs and he was getting exceedingly hot, which was surprising, since the sun had gone behind the clouds momentarily. Was there a hint of white lacy gusset as she moved? And did she cross and uncross her legs to show her bronzed thighs? Perhaps he was imagining it. Faint heart never won a fair lady, he trawled from the far reaches of his mind. Now is the time to ask a pertinent question.

"What happens if I pull this?" he said, taking one slip from the front of her bodice between thumb and forefinger.

"Try it," was all she said. So he did. And the whole of the top of her bodice fell apart in different directions and there she sat bare-breasted. He leaned across and cupped each breast in one of his hands. Don't rush it, he told himself, "make this one moment that will last forever."

Slowly he withdrew each hand in turn and licked his thumb and forefinger returning to the pronounced nipple and gently massaging it. Surely it wasn't the hot sun that was bringing about that russet glow of the puckered nipple? For some moments he carried on gently massaging the girl, but then all of a sudden she swivelled around and she was sitting between his legs and they were looking out to sea. She put her hand behind her and – miraculously – found that the front of his trousers were unzipped so he reciprocated by gently leaning forward and rolling her skirt – very slowly – up the full extent of her thighs and over her hips.

Very, very gently one hand went down the front of her pants and she shuffled slightly so that his finger's entrance into her was made easy. And how wet she was. He was content to stay like this massaging the fold of her sex but things had gone too far and they were both too excited for this to be the apogee of their love-making. She stood up, pushed him back, slipped her panties to around her ankles and sat astride him. For one moment she was still ... then they started pushing together in perfect harmony.

"Wait a moment," he said and he struggled out of his trousers... "Come on me again," and she did and this time he was able to grasp each hand around each cheek of her bottom and draw him to her. His fingers were kneading the inside of her sex and her strong v-bone was firmly thumping into his. There was no pain, just the passion of a seemingly fateful union. And so they went rigid and both felt the ebb and flow of their juices until detumescence took over. Gradually they slipped – or slurped – apart and she lay on him for some twenty more minutes. Whatever he said was not going to sound appropriate but eventually he managed, "That was fucking marvellous."

For once the F word didn't sound inappropriate – it seemed to sum everything up. So they rolled apart and started to dress. All of a sudden he burst out laughing and his guffaws rolled down of the valley of the Blue Hills.

"What are you laughing at?" she said. He wiped the back of his hand across his eyes.

"Listen to the music," he said. "It's Ravel's 'Bolero'."

For the dolorous 'Pavane' had been superseded by the gathering momentum of the bolero. "If that had been playing five minutes ago I may have burst a blood vessel... or worse. Especially the last crescendo..."

"I see what you mean," she said and started giggling. "Yes, there might have been a tragic climax."

The sun had gone in and the Cornish weather, perverse as ever, was clouding over. He looked at his watch.

"Bloody hell, it's two thirty, and Old Misery Guts has rescheduled our arrangements to leave at three, so we had better get a move on. So they dressed and got in her car.

Nothing was said for ten minutes, and then he asked her, "Are you married?"

"Have been, briefly; ten years ago. It didn't work out."

"Children?"

"No." A period of silence. They were nearing the St. Ives peninsula, and his hand was on her thigh as she drove. "Want to stop?" he said.

"I do, but we've no time."

"Pity..."

More small talk and then, "I'll tell you what impressed me about you. It was your instant rapport with John Opie and this morning when I asked you what the SP was, you replied straightaway. It seems that you think like I do."

She interrupted. "SP means starting price. Give me all the information in a quick summary and don't leave anything out. My Dad was a gambler; it was an expression he used all the time."

"Tell me about your empathy with the arts."

"Well, I used to collect things when I was a little girl – the usual girlie things like dolls and teddies. I was a duffer at school at things like Science and Maths, but good at History, English and Art and -"

"Frock and knickers," he interrupted.

"What?"

"Frock and knickers, that's all you're wearing. I was watching you dress and you didn't put your bra back on, it's in your bag. Frock and knickers..."

"Behave yourself," she said. "Shall I resume?" He nodded. "So, I went up to University and got a Fine Arts degree. And then got a job as a Museum Assistant. God, it bored me to tears. Once I'd set up an exhibition, there was nothing to do for three months except press the number counter that monitors the number of people coming into the exhibition. I was a lively young girl, and all that was being exercised was my thumb so I branched out into P.R. and eventually got a job at the Tate in St. Ives. It suits me well."

"Do you get your talent from your parents?" he enquired. It was five to three and the hotel was still four miles away. "Put your foot down."

"My mother was arty but didn't have the opportunity to express herself. She and my father split up when I was small... I don't think they were married. She died when I was in my teens, and I haven't heard from my father for years. I don't know a lot about him. I'd heard he was quite a reputable dealer but, as I say, I haven't heard from him for years. You said that you were once a dealer; perhaps you may have met him. His name was Sean Beach."

Before he could comment, the car screeched to a stop outside the portico of the Tregunna Castle Hotel. It was three o'clock precisely, and the taxi had just arrived to take the party home. Sir Michael jumped out of the passenger door and leaned over and kissed Sinead.

"I'll be in touch," he said.

He threw himself straight into the taxi, accompanied by a tearful look from Sinead and a withering glower from Sir Patrick. The *Western Morning News* had a nice spread on the Tate extensions and the Terry Frost retrospective, organised by the P.R.O. of the Tate St. Ives, and there was a nice photo of Sir Michael Oliphant, centre-stage with a beautiful girl at his shoulder. It was the girl he had just called 'frock and knickers'. The weather had closed in and there was the famous Cornish mizzle threatening to embrace everything, and he pondered if the weather had been like it was now at ten o'clock this morning, would the happening have happened? Perhaps they would have gone to Truro Museum instead?

The weather on the diesel back to St. Erth was like the London smog of the 1950s. Carbis Bay had disappeared into the mither, and Leland Saltings were now just a sea of mud whereas, previously they were bestrode by a legion of long-legged sea birds. Within minutes it was, "St. Erth – change here for Lunnon – change here for Lunnon – you've gotta change here anyway cos we ain't got any more track."

The journey on the express into Paddington was characterised by stilted conversation, and accompanied by the snorting of GvH as he caught up with his sleep owing. He looked like a corpse huddled in the corner and Sir Michael wished he was one.

They arrived in London to the phone hacking row which meant that Sir Michael was involved in accordance with his 'Media' brief. There were also corruption allegations concerning the 2012 Olympics, which concerned his 'Sport' brief. But these would be small fry if ever the headline became 'Minister took £80,000 bung'.

Sir Michael mused that his problems started with WEFADA. These noble letters stood for the West End Fine Art Dealers Association, but as he doodled he came up with an alternative acronym which was 'Well, Everything's Fucked and Decidedly Awkward'.

The following morning at ten thirty, a re-fragranced George van Hesselinck was ushered into his office.

CHAPTER EIGHT

"TELL ME, CAN YOU ALSO ORGANISE...?"

"Come in, George, nice to see you again," Sir Michael lied.

He shook hands with GvH, motioned to him to sit down and his eyes took George's to the internal camera and microphone of the building's CCTV. This interview had to be business-like, for everything was recorded for posterity. It was a short meeting.

"George, I would like you to act as fine art advisor and consultant to this department at a salary of £100,000 a year. My Department has some legislation pending in Parliament and in Brussels, and we need an advisor of your stature. Please accept".

That was it; GvH accepted with alacrity and Sir Michael Oliphant breathed a sigh of relief. But it did not keep GvH away for long.

Two days later, Sir Michael was intercepted on the way to the office and GvH said, "Take me to lunch, Mike – somewhere al fresco, away from any cameras or microphones."

"We'll dine al fresco on the Embankment."

After lunch, GvH said to Sir Michael, "That £100,000 p.a. will tide me over, but I'll only get paid once a month so I'll need some capital to make inroads into my substantial debts. And I've worked out that your Picasso cartoon could be just the jobbo."

It was with a heavy heart that evening that he took it down off the wall – he had owned it for some twenty years, and tears welled in his eyes. He wrapped it in sheets of brown paper, and at a pre-arranged time met GvH the following day and handed it over.

A week later Sir Michael was hijacked as he walked to the Ministry early morning.

"I got £1.25 million for the Picasso cartoon which has been enough to assuage a group of particularly nasty people who have been harassing me but, unfortunately, I need more…"

"George, this can't go on. I know that I am in thrall to you regarding the Ackroyd-in-Nidderdale auction, but it was a long time ago and you're sucking the life-blood from me."

He looked sideways at GvH to appeal to his better nature, but it appeared to Sir Michael that GvH just did not have a better nature.

"That's the way it is," said GvH firmly. "I've no alternative. You are a knight of the realm and I am sure you must be loaded. And I set you up by giving you a massive backhander. If you can help me find Sean Beach, then I'll lean on him for a substantial wedge of his drug money. After all, my £80,000 probably kick-started that particular avenue of his income. In the meantime, I'm looking to you to drag me out of this mess I'm in."

Sir Michael seethed. Sir Patrick had arranged an office in the Ministry for his new 'artistic advisor' but his proximity plus other continuing problems with his media and sport responsibilities were having an effect on his physical and mental health. And it would not be long before GvH would be shown to be completely out of his depth as an artistic advisor, and political questions might start being asked by his ministerial 'shadow'. So one day he took a bottle of Chianti into Green Park and lay on the grass to consider a way out of the impasse. He swigged the lot and looked at the empty bottle. It was time for the GvH predicament to be faced.

He had contrived for GvH to fall in love with Colin Fetteringham, a delicate customer of Michael's from years back, and he had moved in with him. If he thought this new love would get GvH off his back, then he was sorely wrong. He was left alone to deal with all his other departmental problems for just two weeks, and then GvH was back again. But this time the Chianti in Green Park had enabled him to concoct a believable scenario that he put to GvH. He had paid a private detective to go to Spain and look for Sean Beach – and he had succeeded! He met GvH at the Embankment Cafe and gave him £1,000 in Euros, which he had withdrawn from his bank that morning.

"Sean has sent this to help an old friend."

Far from being grateful, GvH took the money and said, "Is that all I am worth to him? And it's in bloody Euros."

Michael did not comment but added, "He's coming over in three week's time, George, and I'll arrange a meeting – just the three of us – and we'll sort you out once and for all."

It was a Freudian slip when he said that he would sort GvH once and for all, but the Chianti bottle had come to its conclusion that this was the only conclusion to the GvH problem. There was no alternative.

The following morning, Sir Michael Oliphant startled the night security staff at the Ministry by turning up for work at five o'clock in the morning. The Minister for Culture, Media and Sport had cleared a mountain of paperwork when coffee arrived around mid-morning. He was quite pleased with the tricky decisions that he had made, some of which he had been putting off for some time due to the GvH business. This was another aspect of the matter that had been annoying him, for he had hitherto been known as a very efficient minister and, just lately, he knew that he had not been pulling his weight. Three times he had met the Prime Minister informally and he had told him that he wanted to "have an hour alone with him" when both their diaries allowed it. Sir Michael had reckoned that it could not have been vital but it was a matter of concern to him. So he drained his coffee cup and pressed the buzzer for his personal assistant.

"I'm off," he said. "Tell Sir Patrick that there's enough in the pending tray to keep the staff busy for today and tomorrow morning I shall be in at sparrow-fart as usual. The P.M. is threatening me with an interview, so if he gets in touch tell him I'm away on personal business and my phone will be switched off."

So he slipped down the back stairs into Whitehall and walked briskly up to Whitcombe Street, where he hired an Audi for twenty four hours. He paid on his card and immediately regretted it. Sod it, he told himself, should have paid cash.

He calculated how much fuel he might need and pulled into the first garage that he came to. Traffic was light. He knew many of the back-doubles and, as it was mid-morning, he was on the M1 within half –an hour. He put the Audi into cruise control and did a steady 70 mph, as he did not want to pick up a speeding ticket. There were two reasons for this; one was that it would reflect badly that a Cabinet Minister didn't abide by government rules, and the other was that he was on a nefarious mission and was not wanting an interview with Plod under any circumstances.

His steady driving did not endear him to his fellow –travellers, for one passed him on the inside and gave him the wanking sign. He did not respond, and within two hours of driving up the M1 he had reached Junction 29, so he turned off and headed into the Peak District.

It was as if he had never been away. The intervening years had been seemingly timeless; the scenery was as beautiful as ever and the bubbling streams so vibrant and clear. For one moment he wondered what he was doing working in London. Reg the Runner's smallholding still nestled attractively into a fold in the hills west of Matlock. And was that the same goat acting as Security Officer? He knew that they lived to a good age. He dropped the catch on the gate and carefully worked out the radius of Gerald the goat's – if it was the same Gerald – chain and skirted the field and walked towards the luxury caravan in the corner of the field behind the building. He seemed to remember that Reg had told the rates revenue officer that it was a pigsty.

As he turned the corner, Reg came out to meet him. He was redder, fatter and balder, but the twinkle in his eye was still as bright and he put his arms around Michael's neck and hugged him tightly. He couldn't think of any appropriate thing to say so he enquired, "Is it the same goat, Reg?"

"It is, sir, name of Gerald, and sure, he hasn't cost me a penny over all the years. And I have to say the goats scared them all away. Haven't seen a Council man for years... Come inside, sir, let me look at you. Well, the years have been kind to you; you look swell. And on time to the minute, just as you always were. And it's been good to see your progress in Parliament – you always were the most decent, likeable, knowledgeable of men as an antiques dealer, and you seem to have had the same approach in your new profession." At last he paused. "Bushmills, sir?" he said, and poured two large measures, which were downed without a moment's hesitation. There was an awkward silence for just a few moments.

"How's business, Reg? I know the trade had gone arse-upwards but I've no doubt that you still get a decent living. I got out at the right time but I never thought that minimalism would oust the beautiful period, Regency and Victorian and Edwardian furniture and objects – but, by Golly it has. And the pictures that the big auction rooms peddle now... Where have the beautiful landscapes and genre scenes gone? Reg, these are questions that have no answer. How do you make a living these days?"

Reg refilled the two glasses and these were downed which Michael instantly regretted since he had to journey back to London.

"Well, I still do a bit of knocking, a bit of portering and there's always the odd Sexton Blake, but my outgoings are low, the goat keeps himself and I've a smattering of livestock – it's not as good as the old days but I get by. You could say that inflation, deflation, bank rates and Brussels all pass me by. But sir, pleased as I am to see you, I know that you have not driven all this way to enquire after my health, or whether it's the same goat... Tell me why you're here."

Michael fixed him with a steely look that was slightly misted-over due to the Bushmills. He shuffled his tub chair forward on its castors and out his hand on Reg's shoulder. By inclination, he looked beyond him to see if there was any hint of CCTV or microphone – surely not in a caravan in a field in rural Derbyshire?

"Reg," he said. "When I was in business, you could organise anything and everything. Cuban mahogany, bog oak, monkey wood, portering, sexton blaking, buying, selling, labouring. Reg, you could organise anything…"

"And I still can, sir. Anything. But I have to be careful, of course these days, as there are – how shall I put it, sir? – a lot of sophisticated methods around to deny a poor country boy from Ireland a decent living."

Sir Michael smiled, since he had never heard so many anachronisms in one sentence.

"Tell me, Reg," said Sir Michael Oliphant, K.B.E., O.M., B.A. (Hons), Her Majesty's Minister for Culture, Media and Sport. "Tell me, Reg, can you also organise an assassination?"

CHAPTER NINE

"WHAT'S THE CRAIC?"

"What's the craic, sir?" said Reg the Runner, which is the Gaelic version of "what's the SP?" He did not seem at all phased or taken aback for a peremptory request to arrange a murder. He could fix anything.

"The craic – as you so delightfully put it, Reg – is this. I need someone taking out of circulation – someone who will continue to cause me problems as long as he is on this earth drawing breath. I must remain far distant from the deed, but this man must be sent up to heaven – or whatever other place he qualifies for – as soon as possible. There is no alternative. I know you will probably ask if every avenue has been explored. Well, Reg, I have wrestled with all the possibilities about aborting my difficulties with this man, but I have come down unequivocally with the solution that death is the one way out of the conundrum. And an early death at that. Can you arrange it for me? There is decent money available."

Reg lit a Capstan Full Strength. "Who is it, sir?" he asked taking an enormous pull at his cigarette.

"It is someone you met fleetingly some years ago. Funnily enough, my difficulties stem from the time you met him, although you played no part in it of course." He paused for emphasis. "It's George van Hesselinck."

Reg took another deep draw on his Capstan Full Strength, and didn't bat an eyelid.

"Well, I won't ask the reason why this man must be put six foot under God's earth, but I must admit the name surprises me. I am sure that Mr Hill, Mr Ladbroke or Mr Coral would give long odds had they been asked to make a book. And the money, sir?"

Michael looked Reg straight in the eye.

"Reg, in our long relationship we have never bargained over anything. I doubt that there is a going rate for the job. You tell me how much and the money's yours."

There was an ethereal silence, during while he looked round the caravan; nothing bought new, for Reg did not believe in capital expenditure, and everything came from auctions or house clearances.

"Have another whiskey, sir. I am going to close my eyes and think over the matter for as long as it takes."

He leaned back and ostensibly disappeared in the deep feather-filled cushions of the Knole settee. He closed his eyes and, at one time, Michael had thought he had fallen asleep except that he continued to draw on his Capstan Full Strength. He stayed supine for a considerable length of time; Sir Michael stayed silent and the air was still save for the distant jangling of the goat's chain. After twenty minutes, Reg sat bolt upright.

"I'll do it, sir. I know just the man, It'll cost you £50,000 – all I need is the address of Mr. George van Hesselinck."

"It's 17 Colville Mansions, Kensal Rise," he said, taking a large brown envelope from his pocket. He had not doubted for one moment that Reg would be able to fix it; he had even had a good stab at the price and got very close to it. He thought it may have been more, so he was more than happy at £50,000. He shook Reg's hand.

"Here's £30,000. The balance will be brought to you when I hear about the unfortunate demise of GvH. Have you any idea of the time schedule, Reg?"

"Straightaway; the job will be done within two weeks."

"Great," thought Sir Michael, "I won't need to stall on the putative meeting with Sean Beach; a meeting which, given my undoubted organisational skills, I would have had extreme difficulty in bringing to fruition." He had been with Reg for under an hour but felt so pleased that it was almost as if the job had been done. He turned down the offer of another Bushmills.

"I must be exceedingly careful," he said. A quick handshake and a hug and he was through the door of the caravan. He slipped down the upturned crates that served as caravan steps, recovered his composure but then misjudged the radius of Gerald the Goat's chain and had to do an Irish jig, appropriately, to avoid getting to know Gerald's horns better. He got into his hire car and carefully, very carefully drove along the country lanes for he knew that he was over the drink drive limit. He stopped at the first greasy spoon café that he came to and ordered an enormous all day breakfast. He judged that he had been on the go for over twelve hours, and calculated that all he had partaken all day was a cup of coffee at the Ministry and half a bottle of Bushmills with Reg. The food had the effect of satisfying his hunger and negating Reg's Bushmills, but after another fifty miles on the road he felt his eyelids lowering so, without any more delay, he booked into a first class hotel and slept for ten hours solid. Despite the previous day's promise, he was not behind his desk at sparrow-fart.

It took Reg two days to tie up his loose ends, chief among them sorting the well being of his trusty servant, the goat. He put £20,000 of the money into his safe and the other £10,000 in his back pocket.

Early in the morning he drove carefully to Fishguard, parked his car and got on the Dublin ferry. He had a false passport in the name of Eugene Brannigan and he had no problem in entering the Irish Republic for no one looked more Irish than Reg. He booked into Carole Kenworthy's digs, where he often stayed during his knocking expeditions, freshened up, and later that evening sauntered along to Humpty Dan's Bar in McCann Street, a seedy pub that had kept the Fenian atmosphere for the tourists. The old Republican songs were belted out in the background, and one room even had a spittoon on the floor and sawdust in the corner. Quite a few of his friends from his childhood were there and much Guinness was consumed.

Throughout the evening he continually patted his back pocket which was fastened by a big overcoat-sized button and Velcro. On or about the sixth Guinness, he realised that his back-pocket cash was in sterling whereas the Republic's currency was in Euros, but it did not unduly concern him, since the pound was in ascendancy with the Euro at that time. A mere detail, he told himself and did not foresee that this 'business arrangement' would be jeopardised.

At ten o'clock, the man who he was waiting for came into the bar and he recognised Reg straight away.

"What are you doing here, Reg – or is it Eugene? I thought the knocking game was finished, as nobody wanted brown furniture anymore?"

"No they don't," was Reg's reply. "But I haven't come over for the knocking. I have come to see you."

The man was Liam Fogarty; even before the troubles he was known as a hard man, and the years had not softened the edges. He had been arraigned for several murders and kneecappings but no judge or jury would convict him and, like Al Capone in the thirties America, his criminal record was negligible. It was to everyone's relief that the tension seemed to be over for nobody messed with Liam Fogarty. He had even set up a window cleaning round, although no one saw him go out much. He was known to be knocking off the widow Murphy at number 319.

"Have a pint, Liam. I may have some business to put your way."

"You don't want me to come to Derbyshire to clean your windows do you?" he said with a smile. Reg ignored the offer.

"This is your kind of business," he replied.

"What kind of business is that?" Liam Fogarty was playing dumb and obverse.

"YOUR kind of business... but I don't want to talk about it here." He pushed a pint of Guinness towards Liam Fogarty and took a deep draught of his own. "Meet me tomorrow morning at ten o'clock in St. Aloysius Park, near the fountain. It will be worth your while."

"Can you not give me a hint?" But the conversation was terminated by a shout from near the bar.

Liam Fogarty said, "Reg, I'll see you in the morning at ten. Can't talk now – I've promised to sing 'The Irish Rover' for those Americans over there. They're paying me fifty dollars. What's that in real money?"

The following morning Reg went early to St. Alyoisius Park, sat down near the fountain and waited. He did not have to wait long, for he was studying the runners in *The Racing Post* for that afternoon's meeting at Clonmel when Liam Fogarty arrived right on time and sat down beside him. Reg jabbed his finger at the three fifteen race and said "Do you think that the booking of Ruby Walsh for that donkey of Kerrigan's has any significance?"

"You haven't brought me out here to discuss Ruby's prospects in the three fifteen," was the surly reply. "Get on with it."

"Right," said Reg. "I want a man killed in London. Can you do it? He's not a high profile character, he'll have no security men around him… Easy-peasy for you. He's an insignificant nonentity who has to be eliminated. The money is good – £10,000 now – here in the park as an advance payment and when the deed is done I'll make a quick return to Dublin with the balance of another £10,000."

Liam Fogarty did not have to think about it.

"Oi'll do it, Reg, bit of assassinating beats window cleaning any day, and pays better. Give me the money and the man's details, and the job'll be done within a week." Reg popped the button on his back pocket, released the Velcro, took the envelope out and gave it to Liam Fogarty. He then took Fogarty's hand, opened the palm and wrote 'George van Hesselinck, 17 Colville Mansions, Kensal Rise, North London' and told him to commit it to memory.

"You will be looking for a small fussy man. He will probably be immaculately dressed and he walks, not with a pronounced limp, but with a pronounced mince. I need not tell you about his sexual orientation as it will be obvious. Just one thing – he lives with his partner – a bloke called Colin Fetteringham – but they are as different as chalk from cheese."

Liam got up to leave and turned to shake Reg's hand. Reg looked him in the eye and said. "For fuck's sake, don't kill the wrong one!"

Reg was pleased that there was no incriminating evidence between him and Fogarty unless he did not wash his hands for a month, but Fogarty had got away with several killings by being immaculate with the smaller details. So Reg quit the park, strode purposefully to Carole Kenworthy's digs, booked out, caught the ferry, drove to Derbyshire, and was home in eleven hours and fifty two minutes. The goat was pleased to see him so he ruffled his ears, tugged his beard and said, "Job's a good'un!"

CHAPTER TEN

THE CITY GENT

Liam Fogarty booked into the Strand Palace Hotel. He could have stayed with relatives in Kilburn, but on this visit he wanted to remain anonymous. He had shaved especially for the visit, his perpetual stubble temporarily abandoned. He had drifted from job to job – in the shipyards, at a brewery and he'd sold loft insulation door-to-door before embracing the IRA cause in the 1960s, where he had acquired the gift of killing people. Unconvicted by judges and juries both north and south of the border, he had acquired over the years a mastery of the many regional accents of Britain and Ireland. So when he arrived in London, he spoke a mixture of perceived English with a slight cockney twang. All he brought with him was a carrier bag with overnight toiletries and a small collapsible umbrella, the tip firmly covered with a screw cap. This umbrella had been instrumental in the murder of some half a dozen victims during the troubles. It was whilst he was in Libya, arranging the purchase of weapons and explosives, that he had been offered the unique killer umbrella. The top was spring-loaded and was fed by a small chamber containing compadoxine, the strongest poison known to man. The chamber led to a needlepoint, and death was instantaneous.

He took the tube to North London and sought out Kensal Rise, the home of GvH and Colin Fetteringham. He did not have to wait long, a matter of two hours loitering in street inconspicuously, before two men came down the steps of Colville Mansions and stepped along the street arm-in-arm. He did not have to guess who was GvH – it was obvious by Reg's description. So he followed the couple for a short while until they parted, and GvH went to the Tube station and took the train to Bank station. He went up the escalator, out of the station and walked briskly to the West End. It was obvious that this was a form of constitutional walk for the man, but as he went up Bond Street and turned into the side street of the fine art quarter, his shoulders dropped perceptibly. He took out large bunch of keys and let himself into a double-fronted gallery and Fogarty could see the reason for his sluggish body language. Under the masthead in impressive gold leaf was scribed 'George van Hesselinck – International Purveyor of Works of Art and Objects of Virtue' but unfortunately pasted in several places on the dropped shutter was 'CLOSED UNTIL FURTHER NOTICE'. GvH was only inside for a few moments before he reappeared, walked back to Bank station and returned to Kensal Rise, followed all the time at a discreet distance by Liam Fogarty.

The following day, the same scenario was repeated, only this time it was about an hour later. In fact, Fogarty was about to abandon his day's surveillance, for he felt he was becoming conspicuous but he went all the way to the galleries with him all the time formulating the plan that was to be used. His mind harked back to the 1970s when, on a trip to London, he had noticed that the legion of city workers had been attired in what seemed a uniform of black coat, waistcoat and striped trousers, wearing a bowler hat and carrying a rolled umbrella. This time, some forty years on, there was still a proportion dressed in city uniform.

So the following morning, he came out of Strand Palace Hotel and, instead of travelling to Kensal Rise, he went to Edgware Road by tube. In the plethora of charity shops there, he tried on and bought a black jacket and a pair of striped city trousers. From Oxfam he tried on a bowler hat which was about four sizes too big, but they had one in the back that fitted him. They also had a pair of black leather patent shoes. The jacket and trousers were slightly oversized and he left Edgware Road well pleased with his purchases – he liked the 'craic' of the kill and he whistled a Fenian air as he walked along. He had no conscience. He bought two bananas from a roadside barrow-boy, and peeled and ate them as he walked along. He was careful to deposit the skins in a proper receptacle, but then he had a brainwave and went back and got one out and put it in his carrier bag. He felt rather incongruous carrying the umbrella, especially as it started to rain and he couldn't chance putting it up. He returned to the Strand Palace

Hotel, unpacked his purchases and hung them in his wardrobe. He went out and had a pizza, which he ate on Westminster Bridge, and all the time he was working out the precise details as to how he was going to carry out his commission. In Hampstead, GvH and Colin Fetteringham were dining in an upmarket bistro, but there was a tension between them because GvH had no money and Colin was beginning to tire of hearing about the millions that GvH had earned and the big deals that he had done when now he couldn't even afford to tip the waiter. Just down the road Her Majesty's Minister for Culture, Media and Sports was looking at all his media information channels to see if there was any news, although he did not exactly know what he was looking for. Sir Patrick could tell that he was on edge so he kept away. Two hundred miles away, Reg the Runner was pottering around his smallholding with a battered transistor radio by his side. One person under no strain was Liam Fogarty, for a mincing nine stone man held no fears for him since he had tangled with hit men from the other side as well as hard men from the police and the military. He decided that the following day his plan would be carried out. There was no hurry for it seemed that GvH always left around noon, so he had a full breakfast and eventually booked out and left the hotel mid-morning clutching a carrier bag and wearing just a T-shirt, tight jeans and trainers. He needed to find somewhere to change and was contemplating whether the toilets of a pub or a betting shop would be more appropriate, but he came down on the side of the pub because he knew that the toilets of The World Turned Upside Down were just inside the entrance. So he went in wearing jeans and T-shirt and came out dressed as a city gent. He folded the jeans and T-shirt into the carrier bag and put yesterday's banana skin on top of the clothes. Outside, his bowler was tilted at a rakish angle and he walked along with a spring in his step. His thoughts were not at all with GvH who he was planning to send to heaven soon, but rather with the widow Murphy at 319; he was entirely without conscience.

He was early arriving at Kensal Rise, so he took to sauntering along the pavement on either side of the road as far as he dared in each direction, all the time keeping the steps of Colville Mansions just within his view. At his third perambulation – and just when he was getting worried about possible over-exposure – he was almost adjacent to the steps and GvH came skipping down on his own. GvH did a nippy entrechat and hurried along the road, followed at a discreet distance by Liam Fogarty, who shadowed him all the way back to Bank station and on his morning constitutional walk to the West End and Bond Street. He felt more at home in the crowds of Bond Street, but he had honed his skills in the back streets of Belfast and Londonderry and he felt inconspicuous. Fogarty relaxed when GvH went in to his shuttered premises, but GvH spent only thirty seconds inside on this visit and Liam Fogarty was for one moment thrown by this departure from the normal. He seemed to be in a tearing hurry as he sped along the crowded streets with Fogarty not far behind, and they were soon back at Bank Station and on the platform awaiting the tube train coming into the station.

"Mind the gap!" yelled the porter, "mind the gap."

The waiting crowd was perhaps four or five deep, and GvH was just where Fogarty wanted him, right on the edge of the platform. Soon there was the suck of the air into the vacuum of the platform, and the whole structure seemingly shuddered as the whoosh of the train induced an involuntary leaning-forward of the crowd, as it emerged from the tunnel with only inches from the red brick sides. When it got to about fifty metres from where GvH was standing Fogarty surreptitiously dropped the banana skin that he had taken from his carrier bag. He then elevated his umbrella into a horizontal position and slid it between a young lady and her companions both weighed down with rucksacks, and placed the tip of the umbrella into the small of GvH's back. A sharp shove and GvH disappeared under the wheels of the train, and the whole crowd emitted a bloodcurdling scream. Fogarty retracted the umbrella, wheeled round and joined the crowd that was just exiting the train and became instantaneously anonymous. He climbed the back stairs at Bank Station and within thirty seconds was outside the station and in the fresh air. He walked along in no particular hurry, not wishing to draw attention to himself as he checked the side streets. Within a minute, he had found what he was seeking and was crouching down beside an industrial waste bin. In the confined space up to the wall, he quickly slipped out of his black attire and was in jeans and T-shirt again. He slipped all the clothing that he had just discarded into the bin, and then picked up a pile of squashed-up cardboard and rammed it on top. Within half –an –hour, he was heading out of London and on his way back to Dublin. As he quit the Capital, he was aware of the emergency services, sirens blaring and speeding in the opposite direction. He permitted himself a smile and, since the adrenaline was running a bit speedier than usual, he pledged that he just might call and see the widow Murphy at number 319.

The tragedy happened for the *London Evening Standard* to just about abort its current headline and hit the streets with:

TOP ART DEALER IN HORRIFIC ACCIDENT
GEORGE VAN HESSELINCK DIES AT BANK STATION

The paper sellers were shouting out the headlines. By a quirk of timing, the newspaper had pipped other media avenues. From his office in Whitehall, Sir Michael excused himself and told himself he was "going for a constitutional", bought an *Evening Standard*, went into Green Park, took off his coat, lay on his elbows and drew the *Standard* to him, but unfortunately there was precious little information other than the headline – but that certainly sent a tingle down his spine.

The *Daily Telegraph* the following morning had intricate details as to how the international art dealer had slipped on a banana skin and had fallen under a train, which had neatly decapitated him. So Sir Michael dictated a sympathetic letter to Colin Fetteringham, and then called a press conference to pay tribute to this 'international icon' who had made his mark with WEFADA and who, although new to his appointment as an advisor and consultant in the Ministry, had already made his mark.

"He will be greatly missed and our thoughts are with his partner at this tragic time."

There then arose a major problem with the mourning process. The coroner refused to release the body for disposal, as it was such an unusual and tragic case.

"I wonder why this should be so?" enquired Sir Michael of his permanent private secretary when they met to discuss some of the ramifications brought up by WEFADA, notably in respect of the Artists Resale Rights.

"Don't know," said Sir Patrick drily. "I suppose that there are still bits of the little bugger all over the place – you know what I mean – on the train's buffers, the advertising hoardings, in the shale between the tracks, so perhaps the coroner wants to ensure George's 100% all there before his partner is allowed to pour him into the coffin."

"Enough," interrupted Sir Michael, "too much detail. So you don't think it's unusual?"

"Nah," said Sir Patrick. "I bet that every mortuary had drawers full of latter-day Georges, all waiting for the Jigsaw Consultant to call and do a bit of mixing and matching."

Sir Patrick was devoid of any emotional attachment, and certainly not to GvH, whom he could not abide.

So Colin Fetteringham was faced with a dilemma. Whilst he was distraught at losing his erstwhile partner, he was quite enjoying a taste of national fame for the first time in his life. So he went ahead and organised a memorial service, and quite a memorial service it was. Sir Michael attended and recognised a few dealer colleagues from his former profession, although they were a few rungs below GvH in the cultural echelon. He went with his Police Protection Officer Glyn Amos, and Sir Patrick came along as well, for although he disliked GvH, he was still trying to ingratiate himself with Sir Michael after his breakfast table rollicking at the Tregunna Castle Hotel.

At the service and at the buffet afterwards Sir Michael's eyes wandered around the congregation, and it was obvious that two plain-clothed policeman were circulating and asking questions.

He turned to Glyn Amos and enquired, "What are they doing here? Homosexuality is no longer a crime, is it?" It was his weak attempt at a joke.

"No," was the reply from Glyn Amos. "It seemed that before GvH went down the Tubes – and that's a better joke than yours, Sir Michael – there was a bit of a mystery about his life and circumstances. All was not as it appeared to be with GvH. Apparently he was skint and was becoming an embarrassment to the arts establishment. It seems that the slip under the train was straightforward enough, but there are a lot of unanswered questions. That's why Plod is doing a bit of mingling. Apparently GvH has been to Spain recently to find a chap called Sean Beach, a former art dealer turned drug dealer, and Interpol have a file on his movements. I don't think they were close and I don't think GvH had any better luck than Interpol for they've been after him for bloody ages…"

"No?" said Sir Michael.

"I shouldn't think for one moment that Sean Beach will be here."

"No," said Sir Michael.

"But you never know; some people are dead morbid and funerals attract some funny people. And anyway, Plod cannot resist a day out from the office and getting their noses stuck in the trough... Look at those two; you'd think they've never eaten. I think I might slide over there and join them."

Sir Michael looked again around the crowd, for his memory had been nudged by Glyn Amos and his assertion that some funny people come to funerals, for he wondered if Reg the Runner might turn up, although he did not really expect it. But it did nudge his memory that there was a certain balance outstanding, so the following morning he vowed to do something about the balance he owed on a certain job he had commissioned.

He made an early start. He had spoken to Reg, using some sort of code to tell him that he would be coming to "square his account" and that he'd drop in halfway through the morning.

It was all very well to have these sophisticated cameras and telephones, but it made you bloody nervous of everything – even a trip to a field in Derbyshire. The journey was taken very carefully and went off without incident, and as he skirted the radius of the goat's chain, Reg came out to greet him.

"Job's a good'un, sir."

He hugged him. Good old Reg, he thought, you can rely on him for anything. He hugged him and felt a genuine warmth run through their bodies as if promulgated by an electric spark.

"Bushmills, sir?"

"Just a small one."

He slipped a brown envelope onto the top of the television.

"Thanks," he said.

"T'was a nasty accident the man had, sir. But at least the man did not suffer; some people go downhill for years..."

Michael interrupted, "GvH only went down five foot."

That was that. Some trivial conversation ensued and then it was time for him to say, "Reg, I must go – thanks for everything."

They skirted the goat, hugged again, and Reg said, "I suppose there will be a coroner's inquest; it'll be interesting to see what they come up with."

"It will indeed." He got into his car and drove off.

The following day Reg retraced his steps to Dublin, met Liam Fogarty and paid him the balance. He encountered no problems in his drive back to Derbyshire, except that the large button securing his back pocket made it uncomfortable for driving, so he made a mental note to cut if off when he got home. That should bring an end to that particular episode in his chequered career, probably one of the most interesting episodes. He lifted the latch and the goat came to greet him, so he gave the goat's beard a playful tug and said,

"Gerald, the job's a good'un."

CHAPTER ELEVEN

THE BANK JOB

Detective Superintendent Terry Robbins took the telephone call in his office in New Scotland Yard. He had progressed through four provincial police forces, and was now Chief Forensic Officer to the Metropolitan Police.

"Hello, Terry. It's Dr Harbjan Singh, Coroner's Officer to the City of London Coroner. I think you ought to come down to the City Mortuary; there is something very interesting that I want to show you."

"Okay, I'll pop in before lunch, say around midday."

"Not if you want to enjoy your lunch. I suggest that you come afterwards – say two thirty, if that suits you?"

"I've a lot on this afternoon. Is it important?"

"Very."

"Okay, see you at two thirty."

So at mid-afternoon Chief Superintendent Terry Robbins and his deputy Chief Inspector Malcolm Reed, met Dr Singh at the mortuary. They donned all-over white siren suits, rubber gloves and Wellington boots, and then went into a room furnished only with two central slabs, along with a phalanx of what appeared to be large filing drawers against one complete wall of the room. Dr Singh consulted his clipboard and motioned to his workers to bring out the contents of drawer no. 12A.

"We don't have a 13 – it's unlucky," said Dr Singh, drily. So a torso was brought forward and put on the central slab, and Dr Singh turned to his foreman.

"Bring the other bits and pieces and put them on the other slab." Then, turning to the two policemen, he said, "If you want to be sick, there's a sink over there in the corner."

The other 'bits and pieces' were laid out in some sort of order, with GvH's head at the apex of the slab, this head had survived almost unmarked from its altercation with the far rail of Bank Station.

Unemotionally, Dr Singh said, "I think we've got most of him together but the rats may have got some bits and pieces – but nothing important."

Robbins and Reed then accepted Dr Singh's invitation to visit the sink in the corner of the room, and when they returned to the slab he commenced his summation of the condition of the body before him.

"Forget about his head – as you can see it has survived almost intact. The face has got rather a peaceful expression, don't you think?" He motioned to his workers to turn the torso over. "Now I want you to look at the middle of the back, along the spine and I want to draw your attention to this."

Between the bruises and lacerations and the contusions there was a small puncture mark into the vertebrae of the spine and Dr. Singh pointed his stick at it so they could not miss it.

"I want to break off now from looking at the body to show you this."

He motioned to his worker to bring forward GvH's shoes, and a pair of stylish brogues were put on the slab. Dr. Singh wheeled his instrument trolley alongside the slab and jabbed his pointer at the underside of the shoes.

"We have done extensive tests on these and we've analysed everything we've found. There's the remnants of a crushed grape, some mud from his local churchyard – yes, we can be that exact about its origin – there the hint of a bit of dog shit, some talcum powder from when he was freshening up that morning and I'm now going to ask you a pertinent question. What isn't there?"

"No idea," was the instant reply from the two senior Police Officers who were beginning to get bored by this line of conversation, and whilst they were pleased to depart from the examination of the body, they couldn't see where Dr Singh was leading them to.

"What is missing from the bottom of the shoes?" he almost shouted at Robbins and Reed.

"No, you'll have to tell us," they said in unison.

"Banana... Bloody banana. This man's shoes have not been within a plantation's length of a bloody banana. And George bloody Hesselinck was supposed to have slipped on a banana skin before plunging under the wheels of that train. Well, if he did he must have wiped his shoes in mid-air 'cos there isn't a trace of any banana on them. Right, so, my conclusion is that he did not slip – he was pushed. And he was pushed by something nasty. Let's return to the torso. See that puncture mark just above vertebra no.7? Well, we have analysed the flesh surrounding it, and it is completely saturated in compadoxine, a poison with no known antidote and the most lethal poison known to man. Compadoxine is so lethal he was probably dead as he pitched forward. Compadoxine is instantaneous, and we have had to be very careful when doing our analysis." Dr Singh looked across at the two policemen.

They were dumbfounded. "Well we now have a murder on our hands, and a particularly nasty murder at that," said Robbins. He turned to Dr Singh. "Let me have a full report as soon as you can. You've been very thorough so far – thank you. I'm sorry I was so very thick at the start of this meeting, but perhaps the sight of the body threw me askew. I've only seen one worse than this, when a bloke died in his bath and the immersion had been left on. The bath kept filling with scalding water and then overflowing. He was there for ten days before we were called in, so you can imagine the sight and stink of that bath full of boiling remains. Is there anything else you want to mention to me before we go, Dr Singh?"

"Yes, there is one very important thing that needs your immediate attention. The needle that shot the compadoxine into the back of GvH is not in the corpse. It may still be there in the rubble at Bank station. When the Scene of Crime officers first carried out a fingertip search, they were looking for bits of GvH and a banana skin. The needle just might still be there in the shale between the sleepers. It's a long shot, but I think you ought to do an urgent appraisal."

"Thanks, I'll get onto it straightaway," said Superintendent Robbins, and both policemen gave thankful sighs as they left the mortuary.

They had a number of complicated cases on their hands and they had not approached this case seriously enough and had accepted the fact that GvH had been the victim of an unfortunate accident.

"Christ," Robbins said to Reed, "it's a good job that coroner refused to release the body for burial, for if there had been a cremation, then I suppose that and an accidental death verdict would have been recorded. It's a good job that Dr Singh approached the matter a lot more professionally than we did – he's been so expeditious." So when he got back to the office, he rang Dr Singh and told him so.

Her Majesty's Minister for Culture, Media and Sport took his constitutional walk the following morning. He tripped happily across Green Park and at one time nearly broke into a jog before telling himself, "Now, let's not be silly", and slowed down to a brisk walk. He was then stopped in his tracks by the Evening Standard placard which read 'Bank Station Closed. Chaos'. It did not surprise him much, as the booking office staff had been threatening to strike so he surmised that they had done so. When he got back to the office he made a snide remark to Glyn Amos, his Police Protection Officer.

"Bank Station's closed Glyn..."

"I know, sir. Robbo's closed it. They're having a fingertip search."

He then told Sir Michael that it had come through the grapevine that GvH had been murdered and the calm that had enveloped Sir Michael since the incident at Bank station suddenly evaporated and he felt weak.

"You know," said Glyn Amos, "sometimes I wish I was doing some proper coppering, but I suppose I'm better off in the protection squad. Robbo told me he spewed up yesterday when he was examining the remains of GvH. We go back a long way, me and Robbo – incidentally, he told me that he will be coming to see you when the murder investigation gets underway, because he knew that GvH was being paid as an adviser to this Ministry, although I can't see anything sinister in that, can you, Sir Michael?"

"No," was the reply, said in a flat, disinterested manner, which belied the inner turmoil.

"I'll do anything I can to help the investigation."

But he was already working out how to distance himself from GvH. He had been seen with him in his office and also at the Tate in St. Ives. He had probably been seen in Green Park and down the Embankment. He vowed that he was fully immersed in the controversy about Artist's Resale Rights, but secretly, of course, he couldn't give a fuck about it. So, when Robbins and Reed eventually came to see him he stressed the importance of Artist's Resale Rights and bored the pants off the two Officers about the technicalities of the mooted project for over two hours. The two officers departed, apparently satisfied, and mentioned to Glyn Amos on the way out what a drip the minister was and it must be really boring working there instead of proper coppering. It was just the impression Sir Michael wanted to instil in them, and they left feeling that he could be of no help with the enquiry.

Meanwhile, a team of Police Officers were going through Bank station with a fine-tooth comb. The public were up in arms about the closure and Chief Superintendent was getting stick from the public, MPs and Senior Officers at the Met. The banana skin scenario was still in the public domain and the press was up in arms about this cavalier treatment of the London commuter. So Robbins assembled his team at Bank Station and told them he was getting flak from all directions but it was an important job, especially if it yielded results.

"Many of you have been here before. It was a rotten job searching for bits of GvH, but it's not the worst thing that I have done." Then he told them about the body in the bath. "You've all been told that coppering is 95% perspiration and 5% inspiration. We all have some glamorous moments, but most of the time it's bloody tedium. This is the state of the investigation. It has been established beyond doubt that GvH was murdered. As he waited for his train, he was stabbed by a projectile into his spine, and he then fell in front of the train where – to put it crudely – he was minced to little pieces. As you may imagine there are CCTV images of the platform but, as usual, sod's law comes into operation and the camera doesn't pick up anything useful. We arrested the couple of backpackers on either side of GvH but we've eliminated them from the enquiry. We did the usual – picked them up at six thirty in the morning, and kept them in custody for twenty four hours before putting them through the mincer in the interview room, but we knew it was only a cosmetic exercise and that they were completely innocent, so we've let them go. A few other witnesses came forward but couldn't contribute anything, and the poor train driver's still off work with trauma – not surprising really when GvH came flying through the air in front of his train.

"Right – that's the background, and I'll now tell you the reason why we are here today and why Bank Station will be closed for the duration. I'm getting an awful lot of stick about the closure but my back's broad enough to take it. I can't keep it a Scene of Crime forever. And I'm telling you this – unless we find what we are looking for, it's possible that this particularly nasty crime will stay unsolved and the villain or villains will get away with it. So let's hope we get lucky. What we are looking for is this – a needle about 5cm long with probably an aluminium housing and a small chamber at the bottom. It may be there among all the detritus that you see before you, or we may be wasting our time. Now, one thing I must impress on you is that if you see anything that matches my description, *don't touch it* with your bare fingers, as it may have the slightest trace of compadoxine on it. Now compadoxine is the strongest poison known to man, and if you touch it, it will kill you stone dead – deader even than GvH, if that is at all possible. Now, take up the positions that you have been allocated, and best of luck."

Not far away, Sir Michael Oliphant was having a routine day in his office. He had just spoken to Sinead on the phone when Sir Patrick cane into his office and said that the Prime Minister wanted to see him at once. So he walked along the short distance to Downing Street, and was ushered into the Prime Minister's private office. There were just the two of them there, so he was directed to a comfortable armchair into which he was nearly swallowed up.

The Prime Minister said to him, "Mike, there's nothing to worry about, but there are three things that I need to talk to you about. The first is IKEA – Mike, you really must lay off them. I know that you think they are responsible for the decline in the antiques business, but they are major investors in this country and employ a lot of people and pay a lot of rates. Some of the things that you have been saying lately are injudicious to say the least, and are bordering on the libellous. Ignore their presence if you must, but don't castigate them. Okay?"

"I'm sorry," said Sir Michael. "I guess that you are right; it's not their fault. Perhaps it *is* just a change in public taste, but it makes me sad."

"Right," said the Prime Minister, "that's the first thing out of the way. Now the second. The Leader of the Opposition has complained to me informally that you have been less than polite about your Shadow Minister, and mutterings have been heard alluding to her body shape. Can you recall what you may have said?"

"Yes," was the reply. "I said that she had an arse that was the shape of a bag of soil, and I think I was overheard. I'm sorry and I'll apologise informally to her – will that be good enough?"

The Prime Minister smiled, a smile that turned into a wide grin and then a laugh.

"Yes, I suppose she has... It is a curious shape, isn't it? And that is a very good description, but I think an apology is due, so I'll leave it with you to mollify the soil-arsed old bag.... I'm sorry – the Shadow Minister for Culture, Media and Sport. Now, the final thing I want to say to you is this. You are working too hard. You have coped well with all the pressures from your three disciplines, but it is beginning to show, and I want you to take a bit of time off. You are becoming irritable so I want you to disappear for, say ten to fourteen days. I know this phone hacking business has been getting on top of you, and the GvH tragedy must have been a big shock and seem like a personal loss to you. But you have three able deputies and a good staff at the Ministry, so don't feel that you are indispensable. You can take your mobile phone with you, but I am not even insisting on that."

"Prime Minister, I shall do exactly as you suggest," said Sir Michael, so he returned to his office, phoned Sinead and said, "Right, I'm on my way. Put a two week holiday, chit in – or a sick note if you have to... I'm on my way."

He summoned Sir Patrick and told him that, in accordance with his sports brief, the Prime Minister had shown him two yellow cards. Sir Patrick enquired just what he meant by the yellow card analogy, but this was a man who did not know what VPL was so Sir Michael just said, "Forget it." Within the hour, he was on his way to Cornwall.

Progress was slow at Bank Station and, quite honestly, Detective Superintendent Robbins was pessimistic about the outcome. He had sent away for a second and then a third consignment of kneepads, so painful was the centimetre-by-centimetre crawl over the shale of the track. He was more concerned, however, about the criticism he was getting as his designation of Bank Station as a scene of crime ran into a second and then a third day...

They encountered a spell of good weather in Cornwall. They ate well at a succession of attractive restaurants and, of course, revisited the Blue Hills with another bottle of Laurent Perrier and replicated their lovemaking at Trevellas Porth. They took surfing lessons at Trevaunace Cove and were hopeless. They visited the superb Newlyn School painter's exhibition at Penzance Art Gallery, marvelled at the 'plein air' work of the artists and discussed how sad it was that such quality work had been superseded by modern works on people's walls. They walked the low tide to St. Michael's Mount from Marazion and caught the rowboat back. They ate locally landed lobsters at Mousehole and had to quit Padstow in a hurry when he was recognised by an old boy with an, "Aren't you that House of Commons chappie?"

They climbed Tubby's Head, and Sir Michael chucked his mobile phone into the seething frothy natural minehole in the rocks where The Giant Bolster had reputedly bled to death. They attended services at both ends of the religious spectrum at Truro Cathedral and Billy Bray's chapel and raced each other, starting at different directions at Gwennap Pit, around the concentric circles, and Michael surprisingly beat his younger and more athletic opponent. They sang in an open air concert with the magnificent Pool Male Voice Choir, spent a night on Dartmoor in a tent and shuddered when they motored near the notorious prison at Princetown on the way back. They watched stags on Exmoor and a school of porpoises off Land's End. They joined in the local furry dance at Helston and gorged on Cornish ice cream at Coverack. They took Bozza, Sinead's Basset Hound, onto the beach at Porthtowan, and when he tired himself out jumping the rock pools they had to carry him back because he couldn't put one paw in front of another. They got up early on Saturday morning and went to Pool market, where they stocked up with antiques and collectors items, and then took a stall the following day at an upmarket antiques fair at Lostwithiel where they made a profit of

£19 after expenses which they carefully split down the middle and were left with £9.50 each for two days work. They even went torpedo jumping off Walrus Rock and, quite embarrassingly, had to be rescued by the St. Agnes lifeboat when they tried to swim out to the Bowden Rocks whilst only two hundred and fifty metres offshore when riptides were making it one stroke forwards and two sideways.

"Sir, there's something here," came out the cry, which echoed right along the station.

"Don't touch it," was the instruction.

Chief Superintendent Robbins came speedily along the platform to the white-clad police officer with white but mud-grubbed kneepads. He had had three false alarms previously so he was not overexcited by this, but this Officer sounded enthusiastic. Not only was there what appeared to be a tube from a syringe, but there was a small aluminium chamber beneath it. Robbins shouted at the rest of the squad.

"The rest of you take a smoke break." Which, of course, was quite illegal, but was enthusiastically accepted by the search party.

He flicked his stick at the object and said to his deputy "Could be... Radio Dr Singh and ask if he'll come immediately."

Dr Singh was there in half –an hour. It took him only a few moments to confirm that, amongst all the detritus, they had found what they were looking for, so he donned his whites and gloves, took out a pair of tweezers, carefully lifted the item into a plastic evidence bag and sealed it. Enthusiastically he hurried back to his laboratory whilst Robbins turned to his party and addressed them.

"Gentlemen... Sorry, ladies and gentlemen," for there were two female Police Constables in the party, "listen very carefully for this is very important. It appears that we may have found what we are looking for, but this information has to be kept within the confines of all of us down here. For if we alert the villain or villains who perpetrated this heinous crime, then vital evidence may be disposed of. So, as far as the public is concerned, we are going to go along with the banana skin scenario, although that will be difficult with the Coroner's inquest coming up, which will need a lot of careful thought. Thank you for your diligence, ladies and gentlemen. Chuck your overalls in the skip at the end of the platform, and thanks again. Don't bother to return to your stations

– have the rest of the day off on me!" He knocked on the Stationmaster's door.

"You can have your station back, mate."

"Thank fuck," was the muffled reply from within.

They hired a tired old hack and trekked down Jericho Valley and revisited John Opie's cottage, which had first brought them together, and had a day out at Newton Abbot races, the nearest professional track to them. They went point-to-pointing with the Four Burrow and Lamerton Hunts and spent the day eating local pasties and drinking cider but not being the slightest bit tempted by the stargazey pie. They visited the magnificent Tregease Manor, had a meal in the Art Deco buffet room, and watched the goldfish at play in the pond in the garden. They watched an amateur play al fresco on the cliffs above the Driftwood Spars at Trevaunance Cove, and the following night the Royal Shakespeare Company's performance of Loves Labour's Lost at the Hall for Cornwall in Truro. They spent ten hours on the beach at Trevaunance Cove and spent nothing, and then in the evening watched the sun go down over the bungalow in the west of the cove.

The following day they spent a hundred pounds on a magnificent meal at the stylish Penventon Hotel in Redruth. To impress Sinead, Sir Michael slipped back into Government Minister persona and got the commanding officer of HMS Culdrose to give him a personal tour of the Air Sea Rescue Station, including a helicopter ride over the peninsular. And so taken were they by this the following day, and they went to the Scillies on a helicopter from Penzance.

At times Michael felt that there was slight tension, and later that day he found out what it was. They had a delicious lunch at the Tregarthen's Hotel, and to work it off struck out on the path leading to the highest point on St. Mary's. They lay down on their stomachs on the close-cropped hill and looked across at Bryer, St Martins and St Agnes. It had been paradise in the past and they lay and counted the days and what they had done.

"Bloody hell, I've been away nearly a fortnight... Lend me your phone," added Sir Michael.

"Who are you phoning?" was the reply.

"You'll see, my phone is down the hole in Tubby's head, where the Giant Bolster allegedly bled to death, you'll remember."

"Who are you phoning?" she reiterated.

"The Prime Minister, who else?" he said as he punched out the number of the Prime Minister's private telephone. The reply came almost instantaneously, and he said, "It's Mike, sir. I hope I haven't caught you at an inconvenient moment. Could I have a minute of your time, sir?"

The Prime Minister did not seem at all put out.

"Go ahead, Mike."

"Sir, you were quite right. I needed this break and I wonder if I may extend it for a few more days."

The Prime Minister thought about the passage of bills through the Commons and other government business that may involve his Minister, before he said, "Mike, it'll be okay. There's nothing desperate happening that your staff can't handle, and that Sir Patrick of yours is a good man."

"He doesn't know what VPL is," said Sir Michael.

"Pardon?"

"Never mind."

"There's just one thing," said the Prime Minister. "The Coroner has released GvH's body for burial, so I'd like you back for the funeral service. I'll be going myself, but you should be there."

Sir Michael closed his eyes and gave a deep sigh. At last the one thing that had been bothering him had been expunged. What a lucky man he was that the Prime Minister had just uttered the magic words "the body has been released for burial".

"No problem, sir, I'll return in plenty of time. Sorry about the mystery number of this phone – you must have wondered who had got hold of your private number. Well, you see, Prime Minister, my phone is down the hole on Tubby's Head where the Giant Bolster allegedly bled to death."

Then he thought he had better press his thumb on the exit key, leaving that particular conundrum in mid-air along with VPL. He looked across at Sinead.

"There can't be many who have phoned the Prime Minister perched on their elbows in the Scillies. Now, my love, there is something that is bothering you. I've got the Prime Minister to give me a few more days." He looked into her eyes and detected a tear forming in the corner. "Tell me what's bothering you."

"Mike, we've had a marvellous time. Quite apart from the things we have done together, you have regaled me with tales of your former life as an antiques dealer, and while I've been amused and entertained by the tales you've told me, there is one underlying thing that has been bothering me."

"Tell me what it is."

She paused, gathered her breath and looked across at Mike.

"You must have known my father."

There was another long pause. He rolled over from his former supine position and rested on his elbows with his chin cupped in his hands, his eyes were closed to shut out the hot sun.

"Yes, I did, but not well."

"Then why did you not tell me? It must have been a shock to you when I told you that Sean Beach was my father on that day back at St. Ives. So why didn't you say?"

He was thinking fast and wondering how it was going to sound when he delivered it. Some ambiguity was called for.

"Well, nobody knew Sean well. I only met him a few times since we traded on the far boundaries of Derbyshire. Sometimes we met at auctions and he was always there at the knockout afterwards. Do you know what a knock out is?" She shook her head. "Well, it's a highly illegal operation when top dealers form an illicit cartel and agree not to bid against each other for the choice lots at an auction. One nominated dealer buys the items, much to the chagrin of the auctioneers who miss out on their commission percentage being reduced and, of course, the vendor who put the item up for auction would not get as much money for it had all the dealers been bidding against each other. With me so far?"

She nodded. "Well, then after the auction the dealers form a ring, usually in the back of one of the dealers' lorries and they form a ring and knock out the item for its true value. That's why it's called the ring or the knock out. And the dealer who ends up with the item then has to pay the other participants a bunch of money to acknowledge that they did not bid against him. As you can imagine, various dealers were strong on particular items or had a ready customer waiting, so were happy to shell out money to the other dealers. But there was always a common theme to these knock-outs. Sean Beach wasn't the slightest bit interested in acquiring any item; he was only interested in getting money from his fellow dealers. As you can imagine, that did not make him very popular, they felt that he was using them as a milch cow. Then all of a sudden he's gone, skedaddled. He took off, owing everybody money, even the milkman and his tailor and his paper man. He owed everybody, including all the big auction rooms, the Revenue, the VAT man, and many other dealers. You wouldn't believe that he could vanish off the face of the earth, but, by God, he did. He used to have a funny walk which, I believe, was caused by having a misplaced hip as a child. And I know that he was a gambler, big time. Rumour has it that he is running a drug cartel in Spain, and that GvH is involved to a greater or lesser degree and that he has had numerous operations to alter his appearance and cure his deformities. But no one really knows. So you can see why I never wanted to mention it to you. The police came to see me a long time ago because I was on a list of debtors. In fact he still owes me £520 for a Davenport when the cheque bounced. I'm very sorry."

She started to sob quietly. He kissed her to console her and they made love under a hot sky with just the balmiest zephyrs playing around them and rippling the bushes. For two hours they lay in the sun and then they dressed and hurried to catch the last helicopter back to Penzance.

It was to be a tricky time for Detective Chief Superintendent Terry Robbins. It had been his decision to delay the inquest of GvH, and it turned out that his decision had been vindicated. He now had the difficult task of being very selective with the evidence that was put before the coroner and quite what came into the public domain. He was quite keen to hang on to the banana skin.

So, the day after that fortunate find at Bank Station, he took himself with his deputy to see Dr Singh at the City Mortuary. He asked specifically for Dr Singh, if possible, to keep compadoxine out of the public domain, for one mention in the press and the phantom proponent would be alerted. He knew that this would place Dr Singh in an invidious position, but since the doctor was the prime mover in the direction of the enquiry, he felt sure that he would cooperate.

It was fortunate that GvH had no near relatives – in fact he had no relatives at all, neither far nor near – and Colin Fetteringham was too immersed in funeral arrangements to bother too much with the Inquest. Dr Singh was marvellous and dealt extensively with the contusions, lacerations, bruises and the fact that GvH had been scattered all over, that if compadoxine was mentioned at all, Terry Robbins certainly didn't hear it, and the press did not pick up on it. In fact, when Dr Singh's evidence was finished, the coroner adjourned the formalities for half an hour and Terry Robbins wondered if the coroner had taken himself off to be sick. Evidence was further clouded by the fact that the two backpackers had been subpoenaed and had been made to give evidence for half a day, although they could not contribute much. The tactic worked, an open verdict was returned and the body was released to Colin Fetteringham.

Since they had had two days of helicopter trips, the next morning they decided to take the coastal trek from the coastguard station along the cliffs to Chapel Porth, parallel to Man and his Man, and thence on to Porthtowan. So tired were they when they got back that they cancelled their planned trip to the Minack Theatre at Porthcurno, went to bed and slept for ten hours.

The following day they hired a small motor boat and went fishing for mackerel with line spinners in Falmouth Bay. Sinead was quite adept at steering the little boat, and they slipped between the large ships laid up in the docks for repair, provisioning and servicing. In the middle of the bay they ran into a shoal of mackerel and caught eight on the spinner-line so they put ashore into a small bay just outside St. Mawes. Michael found a hollow and stuffed it with bracken and twigs and driftwood – he even found some iron slats to out across the top – and the fish were grilled perfectly. These were served into two long French sticks that they had brought along, more with hope than expectation, and two bottles of Medoc. It had turned out exactly as they had planned, or hoped.

"Marry me," said Sir Michael.

"What?"

"Marry me," he repeated.

"You're crazy!"

"I'm not. Marry me. It has a nice ring to it. Lady Sinead Oliphant."

"I don't know enough about you…"

"I'll tell you. There's not an enormous age gap. I'm fifty three. I started out very young and was self-employed from the age of sixteen, when I had my first market stall. I've been besotted with style and antiques all my life, and the ultimate accolade was when I was bollocked last week by the Prime Minister for having a go at IKEA. Well, the provincial rooms were once so busy that they gave a living to a lot of staff and small dealers, as I was at the time. I use to go to Henry Spencer auctions at Retford every week on the bus, and the drivers were so cooperative in helping me bring my goods back. So I worked hard, progressed up the ladder and created Select Interiors when I was in my late twenties, and it was very successful. I sold out at the right time and had an amazing stroke of luck when I was selected as candidate for our constituency, when I can honestly say that two hours previously the thought had not occurred to me. Remember the story I told you about the Dowager Duchess of Matlock and her immortal phrase 'fucking fuckers fucked off'? I was the youngest ever MP for my constituency. In the Commons I kept my nose clean, and voted for the right leader at the right time in the leadership elections. I've been a Knight of the Shires for the last five years, and her Majesty's Minister for Culture, Media and Sport for the last two years. I have never married and I'm not a poof. As you are probably aware, I'm in rude health as I had a full body MOT only recently, and they tell me that my DNA shows no nasty inherited inadequacies. How's that for a CV? Surely I'm worth taking on? Please marry me!"

"I will, Michael, thank you." She sobbed gently, imbued with mackerel, Medoc and inner happiness.

Rather unsteadily, they navigated back to Falmouth, having consumed both bottles of Medoc to wash down the mackerel. Well over the driving limit, they parked and booked into a hotel in Falmouth, where Sir Michael signed the hotel register rather mischievously as Sir Michael and Lady Sinead Oliphant. The following day, they drove to Mevagissy and bought an engagement ring and, after a celebratory lunch, he drove back to London en route to the funeral of GvH and to resume his Ministerial career suitably refreshed and invigorated.

There was nearly a nasty moment at the Coroner's Office. Colin Fetteringham had turned up with the Co-op undertakers to collect the form empowering the mortuary to release the body. But, of course, Colin could produce no evidence of kinship with GvH, as there were no kin. The official said that the corpse had to be offered to Lionel since he had gone through the partnership ceremony with GvH at the Tower of London last year. But he had decamped to Thailand with his new lover. So Lionel had been contacted to see if he wanted the body but had said, "No thanks, but thanks for the offer." Or words to that effect. Faced with this rejection, Colin had started singing 'Bring Back My Body To Me' in a loud staccato voice in the Coroner's Office. He had fortified himself with a few quick whiskies to guard against possible rejection, but the Co-op undertaker managed to quieten him. The undertaker then pointed out that, since Lionel had abdicated responsibility, the only alternative to releasing the body to Mr Fetteringham was for the Coroner to take responsibility and organise a pauper's funeral, which they clearly did not want. The pompous official then mooted as to whether the happy couple had been divorced, but no one knew where they stood on this matter, so that avenue was not further explored.

Eventually the official signed the release, all the time muttering, "I'm not sure that I am doing the right thing", but when reminded about his responsibilities as to a pauper's funeral, he decided that signing was the easier option. The undertaker and Colin went round to the mortuary and took possession of drawer number 12A and its neighbour.

GvH was of indeterminate religion, or rather, none. The Parish Church of Colville Mansions was St. Botolph's, and it was here that Colin Fetteringham organised the send-off of his partner. The body had been received into the church on the previous evening and displayed on a catafalque in the nave. As Dr Singh had pointed out, the severed head of GvH had survived with rather serene expression, but quite how the body parts under the rest of the shroud were arranged nobody asked. It was almost like a lying-in-state, and to this hundreds of people came to file past and pay their respects to GvH on the catafalque. For the entire time there were two Police Officers present, no doubt to look for the possible attendance of Sean Beach. The coffin had been delivered to the church by a team of coal-black horses drawing a glass-fronted hearse and led on foot by the Co-op undertaker in tall silk stove pipe hat and Colin Fetteringham in mourning suit.

Sir Michael Oliphant was placed in a predicament. He had been asked to deliver the eulogy at the funeral committal service. Many people had assumed that he was close to GvH and, indeed, their acquaintance had gone back many years. However recent events had thrown them together with the WEFADA delegation and his appointment as special advisor to the Ministry. So he agreed. He had lain awake on many nights praying that there was nothing incriminating in the papers that he had left, and was coming up with alibis just in case they were needed. He was especially concerned that there be no trace of the Ackroyd-in-Nidderdale auction. Even these black nights were visited by a touch of black humour as he noted that of the three major settlers at the Grubach auction, only one was now on this earth and drawing breath, and that was him. The other two, Sean and George, had passed to that great art gallery in the sky.

Colin had arranged an impressive send-off for his partner, and it was attended by former lovers, creditors and dealers both big and inconsequential from near and far and from long ago and recent memory. The eulogy used all the adjectives familiar at funerals, for Sir Michael had taken Roget's *Thesaurus* to bed with him one night and had come up with words such as caring, thoughtful, selfless, well-loved and generous. He managed to avoid such words as grasping, rapacious, insatiable, mincing, avaricious and effeminate, and nouns such as Ackroyd-in-Nidderdale, Reg the Runner and Grubachs/Giotto.

The Prime Minister squeezed his arm as he returned from the lectern to the VIP pews and said, "Well done, Mike, you've done the fellow proud."

The hymns that had been chosen for the committal were somehow appropriate, or was he imagining that there was something significant in 'Before thy feet I fall' and paraphrasing it to 'Before thy train I was pushed'? He couldn't baulk at the choice of 'Now my earthly work is done', given the state of George's business. And when the coffin was borne out after the service, it was bound, not for St. Botolph's churchyard, but Golders Green Crematorium, and he couldn't believe his luck. In half an hour, GvH would be just a smouldering pile of ashes.

He went down on his knees and said a prayer of thanks, although he thought it was rather sanctimonious of him for thanking the Almighty for helping him in an assassination. As the coffin was lifted on the shoulders of the bearers, Sir Michael shuffled towards the end of the pew. As it passed, he very quietly said, "Goodbye Sean" as he reached out and touched the coffin, a Freudian slip that passed unnoticed by Sir Patrick, next to him in the pew.

Perhaps a week had elapsed before he announced his engagement to Sinead Travis. At the time, it was a fallow period for news so all the papers went to town with pictures of the happy couple. Curiously, *The Sun* ran a story implying that it "was about time" and came very near to suggesting that Sir Michael Oliphant's sexuality ran parallel to that of the late GvH, since they were often seen together so he asked Sinead to show plenty of "leg and chest", as he put it for the official photographs.

It had never occurred to Sir Michael Oliphant that his sexual orientation was in question, but it was true that, with all his other interests, he wasn't seen much at social events with his latest "squeeze" – as *The Sun* put it – on his arm. He was tempted to take the matter further, especially as the media was one of his government responsibilities, but he thought back a month when there had been a distinct possibility that *The Sun* could have been blaring their headlines about the minister and his £80,000 bung, but he didn't pursue the matter and interest in him, and Sinead duly cooled. At one time he thought that there was a possibility that an investigative reporter may have discovered the Sean Beach connection but they did not, and he considered himself a lucky man.

Chief Superintendent Terry Robbins was struggling. Alternating between his office at New Scotland Yard, the pathology laboratory and wading through dusty files that had not yet reached the computer, he had got precisely nowhere. After the miraculous find at Bank Station, he was in a state of excitement, thinking that there were bound to be fingerprints somewhere on the needle and chamber, and that he would be able to identify them, turn up at the "witching hour" of six thirty in the morning and make an arrest. There was the merest hint of DNA, but blurred and unexplorable and all avenues turned into blind alleys. He then had a brainwave which was not to endear him to the staff at the forensic department of New Scotland Yard.

He put the CCTV from Bank Station on a loop and played it incessantly in the office. One of his staff said he was suffering from travel sickness. It was poor in quality and the only couple who really stood out were the pair of backpackers, and he was beginning to get just the slight pangs of guilt about the way he had treated them. After all, he had arrested them early in the morning, kept them in custody overnight and then given them a good grilling in the interview room. And all the time, he knew that they had nothing to do with the crime, but it was a cosmetic exercise to show the public and his Deputy Commander at the Yard that he was doing something. As if this was not enough, he had used them for his own purpose at the Coroner's Inquest. So occasionally, a feeling of guilt came over him, but it did not last long for he had not reached the rank of Chief Superintendent by being soft.

Colin Fetteringham did not grieve long. He sold anything of even minimal value that Lionel had left, but that did not amount to much. Sitting in his office one afternoon Sir Michael started thinking about whether there may be anything dodgy in his papers, and then had a brainwave and took himself off to the GvH household where he was lucky to find Colin Fetteringham in.

"Could I have a look at George's personal effects, please, as I would like to have something to remember him by."

"You are welcome, Sir Michael," said Colin. "George thought the world of you... Be my guest."

So he rummaged through the papers and withdrew a few items that just may have been incriminating, and took a photo for old time's sake which he put in the shredder as soon as he got back to the office. He put his feet on the desk and congratulated himself on his perspicacity. So Colin left owing a considerable amount of rent, but that did not bother Colin since the lease was in GvH's name. Then he took up with another lover and forgot GvH forever.

Back in the office, Sir Michael ran into another complication when the payroll division rang him and said that the ministry owed GvH two month's salary as an advisor and who shall they pay it to?

"I don't know, send it to Phucket," said Sir Michael and left the payroll division to sort that one out. He figured that there were several debtors after GvH's liabilities, but they wouldn't stand much chance of recovering anything form a pile of ashes from Golders Green Crematorium – perhaps the odd gold tooth or two.

So the GvH investigation was in limbo. So much optimism had fizzled out. There was no family to exert any pressure on the police, and Robbins and Reed and their team got immersed in other complicated investigations. GvH was put – as it were – on the backburner.

And then Chief Inspector Reed retired. The two chiefs had worked together well as a team for a number of years, and their expertise had solved many cases that had looked unsolvable. Occasionally they 'cold-cased' an enquiry and were successful in resurrecting cases from years back, for technology had advanced considerably and they were able to look at things from a different angle. But all they had in GvH's case was a sliver of DNA which had proved unmatchable, and precious little else, and so other cases began to get priority and GvH was pushed further back on their list of priorities. The press and public were left to think that an impoverished art dealer had perished due to a slip on a banana skin.

So the collection for Chief Inspector Malcolm Reed's retirement yielded a sizeable sum, and a party was arranged at a pub in Whitmore Street under the auspices of their divisional commander. Firstly there were the speeches, which contained all the usual clichés, the coppering jokes and anecdotes pertinent to the recipient. Then came the buffet and then the presentations – a framed scroll, a laptop computer and finally a ride-on lawnmower ridden into the function room at maximum speed by the department's liveliest young constable. It was the highlight of the evening, so far with hilarious results – and a compensation bill from the pub's landlord in respect of a carpet that was not due for a trimming. Then the introduction of Malcolm Reed's successor who was to be Chief Inspector Ruari Fallon, newly transferred from the Police Service of Northern Ireland, but known to most in the room as he had been in the Forensic Service for a good many years. The Commander and his wife then made their anticipated early departure, so it was time for the singer, the stripper and the blue comedian. As much beer went down, the party descended into a roughhouse, with tables being knocked over and one young copper being sick over the aspidistra. At two o'clock in the morning, the ride-on mower made a return appearance.

At four o'clock in the morning the party had fizzled out and perhaps a dozen or so – in various stages of inebriation – were seated around a large table, drinking. Some were slurring, some couldn't keep their eyes open, and some were still going strong. They were discussing the strippers' tits, the vocalist who made a complete botch-up of 'Delilah' and the racist jokes of the comedian. And, as is common at functions such as this, the current cases went under review including inevitably that of GvH.

"You're punishing us with that CCTV loop of Bank Station, guv'nor." said one Sergeant. He tried to say 'incessantly' but it just wouldn't come out straight. "What do you want to do, guv'nor, is intersperse it with one of the strippers tits…"

"I wouldn't mind investigating them," interrupted the lawnmower Constable. "The one that is bugging us most is the George van bloody Hesselinck enquiry. I thought we'd swum the Channel when we found that syringe housing. Who'd have thought that we would have been unable to match it? So near yet so far." He put his head in his hands. "It looks like a contract killing to me – but why? GvH had no money, and the Fine Art trade had virtually disowned him and were treating him like a bum. But you don't get a harmless prat off your hands by chucking him under a train." He slurred as he talked and had difficulty in sitting up straight.

"Tell me about it," said his new deputy, Chief Inspector Ruari Fallon, who seemed more sober than most. So he was regaled with the scenario of the banana skin, the melee on the platform, the CCTV on a loop, and the complete absence of any leads until Dr Singh had found traces of compadoxine in the body and they had found the syringe.

Chief Inspector Fallon thought for a moment and then said,

"Seems to me that'll be Liam Fogarty…"

The room fell silent.

These were exciting times for the Minister of Culture, Media and Sport and his bride-to-be. They bought a house in Fulham and Sir Michael moved in. Sinead was tying up loose ends in Cornwall; she had to give three months notice to terminate her job at the Tate in St. Ives, but she came up most weekends. The John Opie was removed from the wall of the Ministry and was given pride of place in their new house. Alongside it hung an aerial photograph of Trevellas Porth and St. Agnes, and they had put a small indentation at the spot where they had their first tryst and they agreed that it was fortunate that the pilot was not taking that particular shot on that particular day. They even managed to identify the hole where the Giant Bolster allegedly bled to death, and where Michael's mobile phone had met its watery end.

They took a lot of enjoyment in furnishing the house in Fulham. They took a lot of the cherished items from his former home, which was then sold, and supplemented them with some new stylish items which they were able to buy reasonably, thanks to the dip in the antiques market. Learning from the IKEA experience, he kept his head down in the House of Commons and tried not to get too involved in anything controversial. The Prime Minister was adept at picking up on the smallest details and wanted to know about the Giant Bolster reputedly bleeding to death in a fissure at Tubby's Head in Cornwall. So he was regaled about the local folklore and how an enormous effigy of the giant was regularly trawled through local streets at pageants and festivals. He laughed when he was told that Sir Michael's mobile phone had been chucked down the fissure and how he had enjoyed his break in Cornwall that the Prime Minister had forced on him.

He said to the Minister of Culture, Media and Sport, "You see, Mike, let that be a lesson to you. Do not aspire to become Prime Minister? Because, if you did, you wouldn't be able to take a long vacation in Cornwall for the press would find you and would follow you all over the place. You certainly wouldn't be able to chuck your phone down Bolster's fissure. Have you tried ringing the number? You'd get an almighty shock if Giant Bolster answered it..."

There were a lot of sore heads the following morning in the Chief Superintendent's office. He had convened a meeting for eleven o'clock that morning to consider Chief Inspector Ruari Fallon's explosive statement only a few hours previously at the retirement party. Even ex-Chief Inspector Malcolm Reed had asked to be allowed to 'sit-in', although he was, of course, now officially retired.

Chief Inspector Ruari Fallon was called out to the front and straightaway asked, "Right, who is Liam Fogarty and why is it him? And how come he's not on any of my DNA checks?"

"May I address the meeting, guv'nor?" asked the Chief Inspector.

"Go ahead."

"Well, if I am correct, the first thing to remember is this man is a professional assassin. The reason that he is not on your DNA register is that Fogarty is a citizen of the Irish Republic. So the first job when I finish this discourse is to contact our colleagues at the Garda. But I have one caveat. This man is so clever, he has been before the courts a dozen times but has always had backup from dodgy advocates, barristers, solicitors and liars, that if he had a conviction at all, it will be for parking on double-yellow lines. And now I want to tell you one earth-shattering fact – this man has killed four of our colleagues. No doubt about it. Dead certain. There may have been more – in fact, it has been said that he brags to the number being eleven. He uses a poison called compadoxine, a poison so deadly that almost instantaneous death ensues. He kills for money, and if this were not a subject so serious I would entertain you by telling you that he also works as a window cleaner and that he is knocking off the widow Murphy at number 319. You see, he covers his tracks by having a regular job, and in that way attracts little attention. He has a little beat-up car, and in the pub that he frequents he is the last to buy a round. No doubt he has money, but he doesn't spend much, so he'll have hidden it in wedges under the floorboards, for he doesn't trust banks, and no bank would have him anyway. He'll be keeping the cash for eventual retirement but quite when that retirement will come nobody knows. This man kills for fun – and money. As I say he has been arrested many time and there's a chance that the Garda has taken his DNA. – all very illegal, of course, but then Liam Fogarty doesn't play by the rules himself. Now I'll tell you about compadoxine. He gets it from Libya – he was doing some gunrunning for the IRA, he was handling explosives and weapons, but one of Colonel Gaddafi's men introduced him to this new poison. So he brought it back from Libya for his own personal use. When the troubles subsided, he weighed in the weapons and the gelignite, but kept the compadoxine for his sideline, although no one knows where he keeps it. There you are, ladies and gentlemen, I give you Liam Fogarty, window cleaner and assassin…"

The room had been silent and there had not been a whisper as the Chief Inspector spoke, but now Chief Superintendent Terry Robbins got to his feet and said, "I suggest we adjourn for twenty minutes or so for coffee and in the meantime I'll contact the Chief Forensic man at the Garda about the DNA. When we reconvene, we'll play the Bank CCTV again for $1,147^{th}$ time, but the first time for Ruari."

There was an air of excitement in the room as the officers sipped their coffee. Terry Robbins had directed that all incoming calls be redirected except for one. Then thirty minutes later came the call he was awaiting from Dublin, and he addressed the reconvened meeting.

"Here is the text from Dublin. There are only four words. It says 'DNA confirms Liam Fogarty'." There was a huge cheer in the room and backslapping from everyone for Ruari Fallon.

When the euphoria had settled down, Robbins said, "Right, put the Bank CCTV loop on again."

They watched it another four times and then Fallon said, "Right, slow it right down… I've got him."

He took a snooker cue and used it as a pointer at the image where GvH had already been circled.

"Bloody hell," he said, "he's dressed as a city gent. You can just see the top of his bowler. Keep an eye on him, slow the tape right down; you can pick him out now that I have identified him. He's inching forward, he's sliding left and right and now there's only two persons between him and GvH. If I stop the tape you can just see the shadow of something in his hand. Bloody hell, I knew it… It would either be a brolly or a walking stick. You can see from the body language of the rest of the crowd that the train has just come out of the tunnel and entered the station. They are imperceptibly swaying slightly from side to side, and then they shuffle forward to get a good position. There – look all of you – GvH is starting to tilt forward, but where's the little guy gone? He's disappeared... The deed has been done. He's wheeled round and is out of camera shot. Right, advance that camera shot, the one from the middle of the platform... There he is! He has joined a throng of passengers that have just exited the train; he's gelled into the seething mass and is walking along unconcernedly as if nothing has happened. The clever fella... The bastard!"

There was another round of applause, this time louder and more sustained than before. Chief Inspector Ruari Fallon put down his cue, went embarrassingly puce-faced and did an amateur straight-backed bow to the cheering audience. The two Chiefs walked towards their private office when the lawnmower Constable yelled out, "Guv'nor, can we put the stripper's tits on the loop?"

Across Westminster, Her Majesty's Minister for Culture, Media and Sport was having a good day. The opposition had targeted him for an attack on one of the disciplines that he was responsible for. But early in the debate his shadow had made a horrendous error compiling the figures that she used to back up her attack. Somehow 1.1 million had become 11 million in her brief, a typing error that had somehow slipped the eagle eye of the sponsors of the motion.

The previous day, Sir Michael had had a meeting with his advisors and other Cabinet colleagues, and the error had been found and confirmed to be the wrong figure, so, "Softly softly catchy monkey," advised the Lord Chancellor.

In the ensuing debate, the opposition went further than expected, and his shadow became quite vituperative to him. Perhaps she had heard the 'bag of soil' attribution to her hind quarters. So Sir Michael led her on and then shot her down in flames when he revealed the figures had been wildly exaggerated. With clever repartee and some off the cuff remarks which had been composed the day before, he enhanced his reputation with a well-constructed speech.

'Marvellous' reported the *Daily Telegraph* the next day in their Commons sketch. 'Beautifully served, fully expounded by a man who has become Prime Minister material.'

Meanwhile he and Sinead had been planning their wedding. Whereas many churches would have married them although Sinead was a divorcee, neither of them had any deep religious convictions, so they decided on a civil ceremony at Westminster Registry Office. Not for them the gimmicky venues, and certainly not the Tower of London with its GvH connections and where he and Lionel had pledged their troth. The honeymoon was discussed, but when Sinead raised the matter, cards were placed firmly on the table by Sir Michael.

"Look, I dare not disappear again during 'term-time'. I was away nearly a month before, and the opposition were getting a bit inquisitive. I've just made a fool of them in Parliament so I'd better keep my head below the parapet for a while. Look, we'll have a lovely wedding day and then spend the first night in our own house, and when Parliament recesses we will go anywhere in the world. You decide, I'll pay. Fair enoughski?" he asked

"Fair enoughski!" was the reply.

So they embroiled themselves in all the complicated arrangements for the nuptials. He did not realise that there was so much to do.

Once he said to Sinead in a light-hearted manner, "If I'd known it was so complicated, I don't know if I would have bothered…"

He realised that he had gone too far and tried to apologise, but she sulked for three days.

CHAPTER TWELVE

PARTITION AND POTATOES

After the euphoria of identifying GvH's assassin, a period of calm returned to the Forensic Department of New Scotland Yard as Chief Superintendent Terry Robbins and his deputy considered their next move. It was imperative that Liam Fogarty's name was not bandied around and became public knowledge, so his name was forbidden to be used and he was to be referred to as 'that man'. The lawnmower Police Constable suggested that the soubriquet 'the bastard' be used, but the Chief decided that he was to be referred to as 'that man'. If Fogarty's name was mentioned, it triggered a £10 donation to the charity fund.

Then the problems and difficulties surfaced, and the Chief and his deputy summarised them. 'That man' was a citizen of the Irish Republic, and if extradition proceedings were started then a prima-facie case would have to be made out. This would mean that Fogarty would be alerted, and out of the window would go the compadoxine and any tainted money. No court would extradite him on the basis of a blurred CCTV tape from Bank Station which, after all, was the only evidence against him. And it was only Ruari Fallon's word that the pinstriped man was him anyway…

The Fogarty team of Fenian barristers would not have to work very hard to negate that evidence. So, it was decided that they would compile a dossier on Fogarty and Ruari Fallon knew just the man to do it. He was an ex-SAS Major living in retirement in the Republic, who for years had been running a small game reserve and wildlife park in the Republic, so he was brought to London and met Robbins and Fallon in a pub in the back streets. He was told to get all the facts on 'that man' and that speed was of the essence. Within days he was back and his report was being eagerly studied.

It was comprehensive. "I've enjoyed doing it," he said "I wouldn't like to go back to the days of the troubles, but it is nice to have some real work to do instead of indulging the mating habits of swans, geese and ducks and studying the faeces of otters to build up a trail and a map of their nightly perambulations. As you said I must, I remained completely anonymous. I spoke to lots of friends and some of the enemies – and, believe me, there are lots more of the latter. I was with a lady in Baltoney Street when 'that man' came to clean the windows and I made the cup of tea that the old girl gave him when he finished. How's that for infiltration? I feel I know everything about 'that man'. He even bought me a pint of Guinness in Humpty Dan's bar. He thought I was an American tourist and I could persuade a party of Yanks to commission him to sing 'The Wild Rover' and, believe me, no Guinness tasted sweeter. Here's what I have found out about him."

He took Robbins and Fallon step-by-step through his dossier. But it made depressing reading – the only light parts were the bits about the window cleaning and his occasional visits to the widow Murphy at number 319. Most of what they read only confirmed that he was firmly entrenched in the Republic, and it made depressing reading. It seemed that it was going to be a monumental task to dislodge him. Shoulders slumped.

"You know" said the ex-SAS Major, "I am as keen to bring him to justice as you are. Some of his victims were old buddies of mine, personal friends over the years, and it's for sure that he played a major part in their deaths, just as he did to your colleagues." There was silence then.

"I've left the best till last."

"What is it? There's nothing in this dossier that excites me."

"It's not written down. I'm going to give you the good news verbally."

"Tell me, for fuck's sake, tell me, and quickly!"

"Your man has a small cottage in the hills; it's no more than a bothy really. He often disappears for a couple of nights there for a spot of hunting and fishing. He usually calls at the widow Murphy for a quick shag on the way, but that doesn't delay him – he's in and out quickly, if you know what I mean! The cottage is very well fortified."

"Well?"

"Here's the news you've been dying to hear and I've been dying to tell."

"Get to the point for fuck's sake. Get to the bloody point."

"The cottage is over the border – it's in Ulster. I would assess that it's over the border by about three hundred yards, but it is definitely three hundred yards inside the United Kingdom."

Detective Superintendent Terry Robbins and Detective Inspector Ruari Fallon felt simultaneously a tremor run down their spine.

"Wow," they said together.

The news was relayed to the rest of the Forensic Department and Terry Robbins could not resist announcing the news in the same way that the ex-SAS man had announced it to him and Ruari. As he said "three hundred yards inside the United Kingdom" there were wild cheers.

Within two days, a task force had been assembled headed by Sergeant Bob Lomas, a former member of the firearms squad. It consisted of four men seemingly set for a fishing and stalking holiday in Northern Ireland. There were no shortage of volunteers. A twenty-year-old Landrover Discovery was acquired and the roof-rack was overflowing with waterproofs, tents, keep-nets, rods and other outdoor paraphernalia chucked randomly on top as would be consistent with four men on holiday together. The coppering equipment of CS gas-spray, truncheons, handcuffs, plastic evidential bags and tasers were loaded carefully in a box and stowed inside. A code had been worked out that the ex-SAS man, who had returned to the province, would text 'that man's here now' as Fogarty neared his cottage. The party had been poring over Google images of the area and Ordnance Survey maps, so that they knew in their own minds the exact environment of the area and the cottage in particular. The only thing they did not know was when Fogarty might arrive, since he seemed to use the cottage "on a whim" – there was no pattern to his visits.

On the morning of the departure of the party, Chief Inspector Ruari Fallon came into the office clutching a Tupperware box under his arm.

"What you got there, guv'nor?" shouted the lawnmower Constable.

"Leprechaun sandwiches." He was always being taunted for his Irishness, but took it in good part.

He said nothing but motioned for Sergeant Bob Lomas to follow him into the office, and to lock the door after him. He slid a side-table towards him and placed a linen square on it. From his drawer he took a diaphanous plastic bag and Sergeant Lomas could see there were a pair of tweezers inside which Fallon carefully withdrew once he had put a pair of gloves on. Taking the Tupperware box, he snapped the lid, and Bob Lomas gasped as he saw the contents, for nestling snugly inside on a sea of bubble wrap was a Mauser pistol. Fallon carefully put a pencil up the barrel, lifted it out and put it on the linen-covered side-table. Next, he rummaged in his drawer and eventually found a phial of white powder. He took the cork out and put a generous sprinkle over the handle and barrel of the Mauser. Instantaneously a perfect set of finger and palm prints appeared.

"On this pistol," he said, "are the fingerprints of 'that man'. I knew this would come in handy one day. It was all ready to be used as conclusive evidence when 'that man' killed one of our officers in Crossmaglen, but the judge ruled it inadmissible evidence. And 'that man' got off again, for the rest of the case against him was weak."

He carefully replaced it back into the Tupperware box and pushed it towards Bob Lomas.

"What do you want me to do with it?" he said.

"Well, I can't anticipate events, but I don't think for one moment that 'that man' will invite you in and allow you to search his cottage and take away evidence that will link him to the killing of GvH and may also link him to the murders of our men. He is an evil man, hard as granite and as devoid of sympathy as that hatstand over there. You will undoubtedly meet resistance..."

"So what do you want me to do?" asked the Sergeant.

"Really, Lomas, you are being incredibly thick. I want you to kill the bastard."

"And the Mauser?"

"I want you to plant it on him!"

It was seven o'clock and the Goblin Teasmaid gurgled into action just as it had at seven o'clock in the morning for the past forty years. Routinely, Liam Fogarty made his usual pot of tea and peered through the shutters of the adjacent window. It was raining, so he drank his tea and went back to sleep. A call of nature ensued some ninety minutes later, so he answered the call and went down to get the morning paper. This time when his fingers parted the shutters the sun was streaming through which put him in an altogether better frame of mind. The Wick Mountains in the distance were looking good and clear, but he thought of the local saying as he looked at them. 'If you can see the Wick Mountains it is not going to rain. If you can't see them it is already raining.'

So he repeated the apocryphal adage and laughed. He considered that he had four options for the day ahead. He could go to the Punchestown races, but he had had a quick look at the runners on the card and considered that he might be picking winners as hard as finding hen's teeth. He could join his mates at Humpty Dan's for the day and play cards and dominoes. This option he would enjoy, but it would entail his taking on up to twelve pints of Guinness supplemented by numerous portions of pork scratchings and a double cheeseburger and chips at lunchtime, and there was always the possibility of visiting American tourists paying for some or all of it in exchange for an earthy rendition of 'The Wild Rover'. But this 'craic' he liked to confine to rainy days, and today looked set fair. He was an outdoor man and a day at Humpty Dan's was often followed by a night tossing and turning in bed as the Guinness, cheeseburger and pork scratchings vied for supremacy inside his stomach and bowels – a condition he described as FBS, or fizzy belly syndrome. Or he could go out window cleaning – he had been window cleaning for forty years, almost as long as he had had the Goblin Teasmaid – but since it had rained earlier, the windows became smeared and the rungs of his ladder became slippery, so he was rapidly putting this possibility at number four. And, anyway, the widow Murphy at number 319 was getting a bit fruitier these days, and he did not feel like tackling that today. He was lucky to have so many possibilities of spending his day, but as the first three were throwing up negative vibrations it looked as though he would decide on option number four, which was a trip to his cottage at Ballyhazel for an overnight stay.

Now nearing sixty years of age, he considered that he had been a lucky man. Well not lucky really, for he had had the guts to stand up to the British who he hated with a passion. His comfort zone had been established because he had never been afraid to tackle the Infiltrators as he called them. He was born on the Catholic side of Belfast, and he had had a religious upbringing being a server and an altar boy at his local church. The priesthood was being considered for this bright young lad, and in fact he had spent a term at seminary in pursuit of that end.

An altercation with the butt end of a soldier's rifle changed all that, and when the troubles started in 1969 he joined the local cell of the Provisional IRA.

"What right have they to be in our Country in the first place and what right has that bloody squaddie from Norfolk to whack me round the chops with a rifle butt just because I was walking on the wrong side of the road?"

It was to be a question that was to be asked many times over the succeeding years and many initiatives had come nowhere near to providing an answer. So he bought a ladder and some leathers and set up a window cleaning round as a cover for his IRA activities. He became commander of the 27th West Belfast Brigade and commenced the fight to reverse partition and seek retribution for the potato harvest fiascos of the mid-Victorian era. As his views became more entrenched, so his campaign became bloodier and more erratic. His summation was that his enemies were those who wore uniforms whether police or military, and also anyone whose accent was not as thick as Belfast porridge. He was involved in bombings, kneecappings, assassinations, bank fraud, and blackmail, but then he decided to specialise and just do assassinations. He was called upon by other cells and became known and feared across the province. When a unit decided that someone had to die, the name was given to Liam Fogarty and the deed was done in a matter of days, but on one occasion the victim lived three years before Fogarty got him. It was generally reckoned that once you were on the Fogarty list you did not come off until you were six feet under, or in the crematorium incinerator.

It was during the time that he was involved in an arms shipment from Libya that he came across the poison compadoxine. No one knew anything about it or wanted to handle it, but Fogarty learned all about this noxious substance and it became his speciality.

His name became known and feared by the British and Irish police and military intelligence. He was arrested many times and, in the years when the policy of detention without trial was being tried, he spent nearly a year in Long Kesh and H-blocks. This treatment merely entrenched his position – as it was bound to – and with the support of sympathetic Fenian solicitors and barristers he had, over the period, managed to persuade many judges and juries that evidence against him was insubstantial. No one gave evidence against Liam Fogarty unless they were prepared to (a) quit the province forever or (b) die. On one occasion, at start of his trial, he stood up and announced that he had the name and address of every juror and the following day none of them turned up for the trial and he was acquitted. Reports of police questioning given to courts over the years consisted of just three words "partition and potatoes" in answer to every question he was asked.

In the 1990s, as numerous tentative solutions to the troubles were enacted, he decided to move south to the Republic, and after a while applied for Irish citizenship which was granted. There he acted as window cleaner and consultant murderer. He was known and feared by many, but he settled down to a staid lifestyle which consisted of daily trips to Humpty Dan's and the occasional foray with his window cleaning cart, so it was decided to 'let sleeping dogs lie'. However, the Police Service of Northern Ireland were not content to take this stance, and they certainly remembered that Fogarty had slaughtered four of their men, although Fogarty claimed that it was eleven, but there was no way of knowing the exact figure. In recognition of the Republic granting him citizenship, he occasionally deigned to pay some income tax. But one policeman who certainly was not content to let this particular dog lie was Chief Inspector Ruari Fallon of the Forensic Division of New Scotland Yard.

So Liam Fogarty fried his eggs and bacon and refilled the Goblin Teasmaid. He had still not decided which of his four alternatives he would follow today. He eliminated Punchestown and Humpty Dan's from the list and had almost come down on the side of a spot of window cleaning when he decided that on the particular sunny morning he was a bit too old to tackle the widow Murphy. He couldn't think why he was reluctant to a trip to Ballyhazel, but he certainly had developed a short-term aversion to going there – then he remembered. There was a certain delicate job that needed his attention – a spot of re-tipping and restocking the chamber of the umbrella that had recently taken a trip to London and had earned him a tidy wedge, courtesy of Reg the Runner, or Eugene Brannigan, or whatever he was calling himself these days. He just had to be very careful handling the compadoxine, but once that mundane job had been done, there would be the pleasure of pitting his wits against the cunning salmon in the clear fast-running stream not a mile from his cottage. So Ballyhazel was decided upon. He started loading his rods into his ancient Fiat, a job which rendered up a small complication in that he hadn't been bothered to break them down from their last outing so they had to be set to travel to Ballyhazel sticking out of the sun-roof.

And then just for the craic and the pure devilment of being Irish, he changed his mind and decided to embrace all four of his alternatives. His first call was to Paddy Power, his local bookmakers, where he decided to leave a Yankee bet on the first four races at Punchestown. He usually studied the form, but there were four that stood out in relation to recent events so he coupled them all together. Trainspotter, Pinstripe, Widow Twankey and Salmon Fisher.

"Shall I give you the money or chuck it straightaway out of the front door?" he enquired of Alby Flanagan, the manager, who made no comment as they are trained to do.

He then popped into Humpty Dan's but there were none of his cronies in there, so he had a swift half of Guinness and came straight out again. His first two calls of his rearranged schedule had taken just five minutes each but the third call was to take slightly longer – but only slightly, and he left her complaining when he would not even stay for a cup of tea.

"You see, Marion, it might just curdle the Guinness that I have just had."

This further annoyed the widow Murphy, for her name was Mary. She had once asked him to marry her and move in.

"No chance," he said as he pulled up his trousers. "How would you feel if I had ten hours in Humpty Dan's and came home with a couple of gallons of Guinness in my belly?"

"Wouldn't like it at all," was the reply.

"Exactly," he said as he pulled up his zip and left.

He drew away in his ancient Fiat and, as he did, the ex-SAS major emerged from a sidestreet, this time in a battered Fiesta, for he had changed his vehicle every day since he commenced his surveillance. Fogarty put a tape of the Clancy Brothers with Tommy Makem and was belting out the old Irish ballads with them when he heard the sound of church bells, so he stopped outside the little redbrick church, went inside and took communion. He had not realised that it was a Saint's day, so he came out feeling cleansed and he pulled away and headed for the track that would lead to one of the many unmarked border crossings that criss-crossed the southern counties of Ulster.

His mind went back to the days as an altar boy and server and his brief period in the seminary, and he tried to justify his relationship with compadoxine by recalling the bible passage of St. Paul's letter to the Romans: 'their tongues have practised deceit... The poison of asps is under their lips, whose mouth is full of cursing and bitterness.' So surely this justified his partition and potatoes stance. But then he considered that the Bible was full of anachronisms like turning the other cheek and the contra-instruction, so he desisted in his theological discussion with himself and went back to singing with Clancy Brothers and Tommy Makem. He really could not justify putting himself forward as some latter-day Saint.

He neared the border, even though no one knew exactly where it was at that point – it was undefined and, anyway, he didn't recognise that any border existed because he did not acknowledge partition. He thought what a lucky man he was as he reached the road leading to his isolated cottage. He paid no bills – rates, water, electricity, and insurance had been paid by provincial sympathisers all these years for 'services rendered'. One man who paid the water rates on his behalf was in a wheelchair. He had no kneecaps, but he was grateful to Liam Fogarty because in the early days of the troubles he had been sent to kill him but Fogarty himself downgraded the punishment and let him off by just kneecapping him. The cottage itself was strangely well fortified for a country dwelling, but there was no chance that any minor villain or criminal would venture near it because on the grapevine it was known that it belonged to Liam Fogarty, and that information alone was enough for it to be given a wide berth. Everyone knew the story of the day in court when Fogarty addressed the jury and said that he knew all their names and addresses.

The ex-SAS Major had dropped back about a mile behind the ancient Fiat and he had remembered the thrill that had run through his body when he was on his surveillance mission and realised that Fogarty was crossing into Ulster. So he sent his last text and the same thrill went shivering down his spine when he envisaged the hunting party receiving it.

'Quarry will be with you soon' was the message that flicked across the border. Fogarty put his foot down as he neared his cottage, for the weather was perfect and he was looking forward expectantly to his duel with the salmon in the fast-flowing little river. As he neared the cottage there was an ancient Land Rover coming in the opposite direction, its roof a jumble of canvases, keep-nets, hampers and tents, and the driver obligingly pulled over to let him pass. He tooted an acknowledgement and there was a chorus of "top of the morning", even though it was early afternoon, and a keep-net dipped in salute.

He pulled up outside his cottage, took a bunch of keys out and unlocked the door. He unloaded a couple of boxes and then decided to put the kettle on and filled it up at the sink opposite the front door.

As he did so, the front door was kicked open and someone said, "Liam Fogarty?"

He answered with an involuntary "Yes".

As he did so, the four occupants of the Land Rover that he had just acknowledged burst in and the leader, who was holding a revolver, shot him through the temple and he died instantaneously.

The tasking party had set off two days previously. They were enjoying themselves so much that they almost forgot what they had come for. A hundred cans of beer and strong lager eased their worries, if they had any. On the middle of the second day they were only half a mile from the little stone-built cottage that they had easily identified from their maps, when the text that they were nervously awaiting bleeped into their telephone. Their man was on his way. As they bumped down the track in their venerable Land Rover, they saw a similarly beat-up old Fiat approaching them, so they drew into the side and the Fiat driver tooted to acknowledge their courtesy. The lawnmower constable waved his keep-net and shouted "top of the morning".

They reached a turn in the track that was just out of sight of the cottage so they stopped and took their 'coppering box' from inside the vehicle and tooled up. They did a U-turn and went back along the track from which they had just come, reaching top speed as they neared the cottage. They saw that the door was still ajar and the four men, selected for their hardness, tumbled out and threw themselves into the little abode. They saw a man at the sink filling a kettle.

"Liam Fogarty?" shouted Bob Lomas.

The man wheeled round and involuntarily responded "Yes".

Bob Lomas shot him through the temple and said, "Here's one for our four men and GvH."

The man fell instantaneously at his feet, blood spurting from his head. Remembering to pull on his rubber gloves he took the Mauser from the Tupperware box, replacing it with the gun that had just killed Fogarty, and snapped the lid.

He threw it to the lawnmower Constable and said, "Look after the leprechaun sandwiches," which lightened the mood of the occasion.

He took the Mauser and rolled the corpse of Fogarty into a sitting position. It was easy to do since rigor mortis had not yet begun to set in. He took the Mauser and very carefully wrapped Fogarty's fingers around it in a firing position.

"Stand back," he said to the others and squeezed Fogarty's trigger finger until it shot a round into the cob at the side of the doorjamb.

He took the Tupperware box back off the lawnmower Constable and put it in his knapsack, at the same time taking out a wad of diaphanous evidence sachets.

He stood up, stepped over the corpse and said, "Job done." They all cheered.

"Well not quite," said Bob Lomas. "You know what we are looking for... Anything that will connect this bastard" – and he kicked him in the ribs as he said it – "with the GvH murder. Anything you think is germane, put it in an evidence bag and we'll take great delight in analysing it when we get back to Forensics at the Yard."

The first thing they did was take everything from the corpse, but then progress was slow, for it just seemed that everything in the cottage was consistent with a bloke having a few days away salmon fishing. They knew that they could be treading an exceedingly narrow line if they went back to Robbins and Fallon with nothing substantial and all they had to justify their 'self-defence' killing was that sliver on the needle housing with just a smear of DNA. After a while, they had a beer break and, as they sat around swigging their cans, the lawnmower Constable looked quizzically at the stone-flag floor of the kitchen.

"You know," he said, looking at the fridge freezer which was located on the far wall of the kitchen. "Why should there be gouges on the flags in front of it?" he said in a low voice. "It looks as though it has been slid forward."

And it had, for when they dragged it out there was an enthusiastic cry when it revealed a strong oak cover which protected a large hole in the floor under the fridge freezer.

"Don't rush!" instructed Bob Lomas, "for there may be something down there that we don't want to touch with a bargepole."

The contents of the hole in the floor turned out to be an umbrella with a broken tip, a walking stick primed ready to go, and a quantity of compadoxine. And there were two wads of pound sterling banknotes wrapped in brown paper.

"Gentlemen, we've found it. Be exceedingly careful with all the poison paraphernalia."

They were all carefully sealed in plastic evidential receptacles. It had taken half a day to go through the cottage with a fine toothcomb, and when Bob Lomas was happy that nothing had been overlooked, they set off back in the Landrover. When they had travelled some thirty miles in from the border, they came across a village police station.

Leaving the engine running, Sergeant Bob Lomas produced his Special Services warrant card, signed personally by the Chief Constable of the Metropolitan Police, to the desk clerk and said, "We have been on a special mission and have had a slight bit of bother at the Fogarty cottage near the border. He drew his gun on us, and I'm afraid that Mr Fogarty is dead."

The counter-clerk was agape, so Bob Lomas continued. "As it is on your patch, I want you to deal with it, will you?"

With this, he left. They drove quickly to the ferry where they were waved through security checks by prior arrangement. News of their achievements had gone before them, and when they reached the office they were enthusiastically cheered by their colleagues.

The following day, Chief Superintendent Terry Robbins cancelled all leave and convened a meeting, to which he brought a case of champagne which he paid for himself. Bob Lomas, the lawnmower Constable and the two other men each addressed their fellows, and they were given permission to mention Fogarty by name. There was a twinkle in his eye when Robbins said it was a pity that Fogarty had resisted arrest, for it would have been preferable to bring him to trial. Detective Chief Inspector Ruari Fallon took Bob Lomas aside and thanked him for carrying out his wishes to the letter.

Robbins then addressed the meeting and said,

"This is the news that you have all been awaiting. Following extensive DNA and fingerprint tests, two men have been irretrievably linked to the killing of George van Hesselinck by Liam Fogarty. They are an itinerant Irishman named Seamus Flynn Reginald O'Dwyer who lives in a field in Derbyshire, and Her Majesty's Minister for Culture, Media and Sport Sir Michael Oliphant K.B.E., O.M., B.A. (Hons). Both men will be arrested and charged with conspiracy to murder."

CHAPTER THIRTEEN

GO TO HORSEFERRY ROAD

Chief Superintendent Terry Robbins and Chief Inspector Ruari Fallon attended early at the Ministry of Culture, Media and Sport by prior appointment on Friday, the day before the wedding of the Minister Sir Michael Oliphant to Miss Sinead Travis.

The policemen requested that the three men be alone for the interview and that the whole morning be allocated to "discuss the business in hand", as the policemen quaintly put it.

Sir Michael was not too perturbed about the fact that two senior policemen had requested the interview because one of his briefs concerned an overview of the London Olympics which had wide ranging security implications, including a proposal to install rocket launchers to deter terrorist plots on adjacent buildings. He figured that if there had been any progress in the GvH enquiry he would have heard about it through Glyn Amos, his Personal Protection Officer, and if he had been requested to make a statement about some tenuous link with GvH a humble plod would have been sent along to do the job.

So, it was no particular concern to him when he welcomed the two senior policemen into his office. Truth-to-tell, with his wedding coming up the next day, he was pleased to tell Sinead that he was unavailable that morning and would not be able to join in any discussions on table-settings or bridesmaids' posies. So he seated them in front of him on two original Chippendale elbow chairs while he sat in an imposing Georgian leather-covered wing armchair.

As soon as they were comfortable he raised his eyebrows and said, "Chief Superintendent?"

The bomb was dropped straight away as Terry Robbins took out his briefcase, opened it and laid a file on the desk in front of him. Sir Michael could see – even upside down – that the file was inscribed in big bold letters '**GEORGE van HESSELINCK'**.

Terry Robbins said, in a voice full of gravitas,

"Michael Oliphant, we have come to arrest you for the conspiracy to murder George van Hesselinck. You do not have to say anything…"

The rest of the caution was lost in the red mist that descended over Sir Michael's mind. There was silence for all of ten minutes, during which Terry Robbins attempted to start reading from a typewritten sheet that he held in front of him only to be halted by a raising of Sir Michael's hand.

Eventually he had gained some sort of equilibrium, looked across the desk and said, "Go ahead."

The reply was ordered and comprehensive. "I produce the following items of evidence:-

    (a)   Sworn statement by Seamus Flynn Reginald O'Dwyer

    (b)   Sworn statements by Roger Crossley of Tetbury and Graham Took of Darlington

    (c)   Original auction catalogue from Messrs Miller & Lee, Ackroyd–in-Nidderdale

    (d)   Forensic report on a £20 note containing D.N.A. of yourself and the aforementioned Seamus Flynn Reginald O'Dwyer

    (e)   Forensic report on a £20 note containing D.N.A. of yourself , Seamus Flynn Reginald O'Dwyer and Liam Fogarty

    (f)   Forensic reports on 32 items removed from the caravan occupied by Seamus Flynn Reginald O'Dwyer and containing your DNA and fingerprints

    (g)   Extracts from your bank account, showing large cash withdrawals on significant dates

    (h)   Number plate recognition details showing your car and a car hired by you in the vicinity of the abode of Seamus Flynn Reginald O'Dwyer on the dates set out in item (a) above

    (i)   CCTV footage at Bank Station, London, showing the alleged assassination of George van Hesselinck by the aforementioned Liam Fogarty

(j)   CCTV footage showing you handing George van Hesselinck a package in Green Park

(k)   CCTV footage showing you handing George van Hesselinck a package at the Embankment."

Chief Superintendent Terry Robbins interrupted his recitation of the list delivered in a monotone and said to Sir Michael, "There are eighty two items of a similar incriminating nature. Do you want me to continue, or are you to accept that there is an answerable case against you and we have full entitlement to arrest you forthwith?"

Sir Michael said nothing except, "That's enough," and motioned that he required time to think and assess the situation.

The Chief Superintendent interrupted his chain of thought by saying, "Do you want to contact your solicitor?"

"No," was the reply.

He realised that so damning and comprehensive was the case against him that there was not the slightest hope of evading guilt – the police had done a sterling job in mounting the dossier against him, they dotted every 'i' and crossed every 't' in compiling their charge sheet. If there had been any other circumstance – especially if it had not concerned him – he would have marvelled at the magnificent coppering. He kicked himself when he thought at just how readily he had supplied his DNA sample at his health MOT, and wondered if he may have got away with it. But then, he thought, there were the statements obtained from Reg the Runner. Poor old Reg, he thought, he must have been scared out of his wits when Plod came to call. Poor old Reg. But his mind was wandering, and he must address the situation as it was. He was, as the old expression goes, 'bang to rights'. His mind was working overtime.

He sent out for coffee and when they consumed it, he said,

"Can I do a deal with you?"

"We're not allowed to do deals."

"Hear me out, please."

"Okay, go ahead."

"As you may know, I am to be married tomorrow. We have no plans to honeymoon abroad. I can give you my passport now, it is in the safe in this office. If you let me marry tomorrow, I shall present myself in your office at New Scotland Yard at 9am on

Monday morning. I would want you to arrange for me to appear before Magistrates at 11am at Horseferry Road Magistrates Court where I would make a statement concerning GvH and another matter. I trust that you would have no difficulty in facilitating these arrangements. It is so important to me that my wedding tomorrow goes ahead without a hitch, and that I may have Sunday to share with my new bride. If you agree to these conditions, in return I shall give you information about a matter that has been wasting police time for twenty years and you are no nearer to solving today. This concerns a matter that can be cleared up by one intricate statement from me. A very important matter..."

"I need to know more," said Terry Robbins.

"Okay. You've heard of Sean Beach?"

"Yes."

"I killed him!"

The Superintendent was aghast. It was his turn to be silent, a silence that reigned for some considerable time before Terry Robbins leaned over and whispered in the ear of his deputy.

Confidentially they discussed the matter and then Robbins said; "How do we know that you will abide by the above?"

"I am a Minister of the Crown," was the reply. "If I abscond, what chance would I have of escaping the law? I wouldn't want to be like John Stonehouse or Ronnie Biggs."

The two policemen stood up.

"You're on," said Terry Robbins, "but if anything goes amiss that would be the end of my police career and that of my deputy too. But I am paid to make delicate judgments, and if there is information about the Sean Beach business, that can be brought to light then I am willing to take a chance. See you at 9am on Monday."

They shook hands and left the office. Sir Michael dropped the catch after them and broke down crying.

It was a sensational wedding, and Sinead looked lovelier than ever. There was not the slightest hitch to the proceedings. Most of the cabinet was there, including the Prime Minister. Friends and colleagues new and old enjoyed the marriage ceremony and the long reception afterwards. Sometime before the ceremony someone had mentioned to Sir Michael that, as a member of the Order of the British Empire, he could have been married in the crypt of St. Paul's Cathedral, but he had considered that it was a trifle ostentatious, but he did not mention it to Sinead, just in case.

The reception went on all day, and the couple took to their bed in their new home at just about midnight. Sunday dawned bright and sunny and, after a leisurely breakfast, they appeared at midday for the photographers in a deal that they would leave them alone for the rest of the day. Then it was a round of the London sights – they went up the Monument, visited St. Paul's Cathedral when Sir Michael nearly let the cat out of the bag about the crypt, but they did take in a service where Sir Michael said special prayers. They packed a lot of other things in and went to bed a lot earlier. Lady Sinead slept soundly, Sir Michael not at all.

Throughout the night he worked out the possible outcome, and it was bleak. There would be no chance of bail from Horseferry Magistrates – not for a murder so meticulously planned and with malice aforethought. A good brief may get him twenty years, but he didn't anticipate any less because we were now talking of two murders since he had traded the Sean Beach scenario in exchange for two days with Sinead. There may be extenuating circumstances, but his political career was now over and could he ask his young bride to wait for him to come out of prison all those years later, an old man? And be tainted by her association with him? No, it would be unfair.

He got up early on Monday morning. Pictures of the wedding were all over the papers, so he left a pile on her bedside table along with the note: 'Be at Horseferry Road Magistrates Court at 11am.' At nine o'clock prompt, he was in the office of Superintendent Terry Robbins where he was formally charged. Just before eleven, he was transported to Horseferry Road but was spared the ignominy of a police van and handcuffs and travelled with Chief Superintendent Terry Robbins in his car.

As it was so serious a charge the magistrates assigned a 'dock brief' but Sir Michael immediately sacked him.

The dock brief refused to be sacked and said to the chairman of the magistrates, "Your Honour, my client will make no plea and will make no statement save to confirm his name and address."

Sir Michael then sacked him again, and this time he stayed sacked as Sir Michael rose to make his statement in accordance with his deal he had worked out with the police. The heaving court had an atmosphere never before encountered at Horseferry Road when, at 11.15am, he rose to make his statement. He told the court how he had been blackmailed by GvH over events that occurred nearly twenty years previously. He said he was dreadfully sorry to involve Seamus Flynn Reginald O'Dwyer and asked the court to be lenient with him. He said that he wanted to clear up another matter concerning GvH with a dealer by the name of Sean Beach – events that were interwoven by a country auction in Ackroyd-in-Nidderdale, and which had eventually led to the death of Mr. Beach, tragically in a vat of sodium hydroxide at his premises at Select Interiors in Derbyshire.

"And I have to tell you that Mr. Beach is the father of my new bride, Lady Sinead Oliphant." He had been speaking for forty minutes when he halted and said, "Can I request a glass of water, Your Honour?" It was brought to him and he balanced it on the ledge adjacent to the dock.

He resumed. "Your Honour, I have had a long career. In my early days I put in long hours to create a business, giving work opportunities to many people. in my subsequent career in politics, I have always sought to fashion my political stance to be fair to all strata of society. Ladies and gentlemen, and especially Sinead, I ask you not to be too hard on my memory…"

He picked up the tumbler of water and took a long draught. He then put a capsule in his mouth and took another draught. He slipped down in the dock and was unconscious before he hit the floor. He had taken cyanide. The court was in uproar. The First Responder was on the scene in a matter of minutes, but he was pronounced dead at the scene. Eventually his body was taken to the City of London Mortuary where it was received by Dr Harbjan Singh.

"Slide him in cabinet 12A," he said to the ambulance driver. "We don't have a 13 here, it's unlucky."

Back in court, business for the day was adjourned.

Lady Sinead Oliphant wept.

Seamus Flynn Reginald O'Dwyer pleaded guilty to conspiracy to murder and was later sentenced to nine years in prison. Gerald the goat was rehomed by the RSPCA. Chief Superintendent Terry Robbins was immediately promoted to Divisional Commander in the Metropolitan Police, and Ruari Fallon was elevated to take charge of the Forensic Department in the rank of Chief Superintendent. Sergeant Bob Lomas was promoted to the rank of Inspector, and the lawnmower Police Constable became a Sergeant. The retired SAS Officer was appointed CBE in the next New Year's Honours List.

THE END